Mail Order Bride

Montana Surprise

Echo Canyon Brides

Book 9

N

LINDA BRIDEY

First Printing, 2015

Dedication

This book is dedicated to all of my faithful readers, without whom I would be nothing. I thank you for the support, reviews, love, and friendship you have shown me as we have gone through this journey together. I am truly blessed to have such a wonderful readership.

Contents

Chapter One

Gino Terranova paced in the stylish parlor of his family home, his heart pounding as he battled disappointment and anger. He'd been duped and he had no idea what to do about it.

"Gino, maybe it won't be so bad," his younger brother, Sal, said.

Gino's blue eyes zeroed in on Sal's. "It won't? What if Lulu had showed up with a child in tow that she hadn't told you about? What would you have done? How would you have felt?"

Sal smiled as he thought about his wife, who was due to have their baby any day now. Then he brought his mind back to the issue at hand. "I don't know. I'm sorry."

Sitting in a chair, Gino put his hands over his face, pressing his fingers against his eyes.

"I don't believe this. I have the worst luck with women. You won the bet and found a wife before I did. Lulu's cousin comes here and she's attracted to Nick and I'm attracted to her, but she's not attracted me at all. Then, this woman's letters came and I really liked them and her. Since we started writing in November, she never mentioned that she had kids."

"I know. I'm sorry," Sal said.

Gino dropped his hands to his lap. "Is that all you can say? Sorry?"

Sal tried to come up with something helpful. "At least she's Catholic."

Gino sent him a baleful glance and got up. He strode out to the kitchen and plucked his heavy, old wool coat from one of the hooks on the wall, and went out the door. He quickly walked to the first barn, needing some time alone to sort through his feelings and figure out what to do.

He decided to take a ride even though they'd arrived home early that afternoon after picking up one Miss Carrie Sheehan, and her daughter, Fiona. As he saddled a horse, their images rose in his mind. The six-year-old, blue-eyed girl with pale blonde hair was adorable. And chatty. She'd asked questions almost the whole way from Billings.

Gino mounted and put his horse into a trot, heading for the trail through the woods that led to some of their wide-open range. He could check out the fences while he mulled the situation over. The cover of the thick evergreens and maple trees helped block the cutting, early February wind as he rode.

It wasn't long until he heard a horse behind him. Gino groaned before looking over his shoulder. His father, Alfredo, trotted up alongside him.

"Are you gonna tell me what the heck happened? The only thing Sal would tell us is that it didn't go as expected. What does that mean?"

Gino and Sal hadn't seen the rest of the family before Gino had left, so they had no idea about what had occurred.

"Pop, I don't know where to start. Yeah, yeah, the beginning, I know," he said before Alfredo could. "Carrie has a daughter named Fiona."

"A daughter? Did she tell you that in her letters?"

"No. If she had, I would've told the rest of you," Gino said. "A kid is a big deal."

"And the girl came with her?"

"Yeah. She's really pretty. She's eight, I guess. I think that's what Carrie said. Blonde hair, blue eyes."

"She sounds pretty," Alfredo said. "How come Carrie didn't tell you?"

Gino let out a breath. "I don't know for sure because we couldn't talk about it in front of Fiona. I don't know what Carrie has told her about why they came here. I didn't want to upset the girl. I think that Carrie is just after my money."

"What? Why do you think that?" Alfredo said, his blue eyes wide.

Gino stopped his horse. "Because Fiona had polio, and her one leg is still paralyzed. She needs medical care that Carrie most likely can't afford on her own."

"Polio! How long ago?" Alfredo asked, concerned for his family's safety.

"Seven months ago. She's not contagious anymore, Pop."

"Thank God," Alfredo said. "Carrie started writing to you in September, not long after Nick and Maura were married. You might be right; she *is* a widow. Maybe her job didn't pay well."

"Maybe."

Alfredo asked, "What's Carrie like? Where are they, anyway?"

"At the Hanover's. I didn't want to introduce you to them before I figure out what to do." Gino let out a mirthless laugh. "Carrie certainly isn't what I expected. The word 'schoolmarm' would accurately describe her. Brown hair worn in a chignon, glasses, and I couldn't really tell what her figure was like since the coat she wore was big on her."

"Schoolmarm? How old is she?"

"Twenty-five, remember?"

Alfredo said, "Oh, yeah. That's right. Is she nice?"

"I don't know. Fiona did most of the talking on the way here, so it's hard to tell. She deceived me, Pop! I'm furious! Just when I think that maybe I've found someone, she turns out to be a liar, and a huge liar at that. A lying schoolmarm!" Gino shouted.

Alfredo worked hard to hide his amusement over his son's last statement. "I thought you said she was an accountant?"

Gino saw the glint of humor in Alfredo's eyes. "A lying accountant then! Don't laugh, Pop! This isn't funny."

"I'm sorry, Gino. You're right," Alfredo said. "Does she need help getting Fiona around?"

Gino's smile was genuine. "She's the cutest thing, Pop, and so mature for eight. She shook my hand and said, 'Hello, Mr. Terranova. I'm Fiona and I had polio, but I'm over it now. My one leg is weak, so they gave me these crutches so I don't fall on my face when I walk.' She moves really well with them, too."

Alfredo chuckled. "She sounds cute and honest, too."

"She's both." Gino started his horse again. "I'm gonna go back in town after a while and talk to Carrie. I need answers before I can decide what to do."

"That's a good idea. Don't be too hasty," Alfredo said. "Now come on back to the house. You should eat and get a little rest."

Gino shook his head. "I'm too wound up, Pop. I'll come after a while."

"Ok, but don't be too long and worry your mother," Alfredo said.

"All right."

Alfredo turned his horse around, trotting back towards their estate while Gino continued down the trail.

As she unpacked, Carrie tried to quell the anxiety that gnawed at her stomach. She'd seen anger and shock flash in Gino's eyes as soon as she'd introduced Fiona to him and his brother, Sal. She knew what a gamble she'd taken by being so deceptive, but she'd done it for Fiona's sake.

Carrie knew from all of the letters they'd exchanged that Gino was a very intelligent man. He must have figured out why she'd pulled her deception, and from his cool manner when he'd said goodbye, it wasn't sitting well with him. However, her first concern was Fiona and she'd do anything to make a good life for her, including deceiving someone into marrying her.

She smiled as she listened to Fiona hum and talk to her doll, Maggie, as she sat on a chair. Fi's good disposition, despite her weak leg, always amazed her. Her daughter had been one of the more fortunate young survivors of the polio infection. Many patients had lost the use of both their legs and suffered deformities and weakened constitutions.

Once her fever had broken for good and her pain and fatigue had lessened, she'd begun recovering rapidly. Her left leg was the only sign left that she'd been sick. From mid-thigh down, the leg had some sensation, but from the top of the ankle down, it was completely paralyzed. The doctors said that there was a chance that it might improve but there was no way to know for sure.

"Mommy, Mr. Terranova seems nice, doesn't he?" Fi asked.

"Yes, he does."

"I like him. He's handsome, too."

Carrie smiled. Fi was right. Gino's light brown hair, slightly hooded cobalt blue eyes and strong jaw were very appealing. He had a great smile and a nice laugh, too. His handsomeness disappointed Carrie. She knew that she didn't appear to be a raving beauty and a man as good-looking as Gino, would want a gorgeous woman.

"Are you hungry?" Carrie asked.

Fi giggled. "Yes. For pie."

Carrie laughed. "You have to have something more than pie."

"Soup and pie. And bread with lots of butter," Carrie said.

"That's more like it. I'll finish up here and we can go to the diner that Gino told us about," Carrie said. "I'm sure they'll have some soup and pie there."

"All right. Maggie would like some hot cocoa."

"She would? Well, we'll see what we can do about that, too."

Fi smiled at Maggie. "Did you hear that? We might have hot cocoa."

It was the simple things that made Fi happy. She got excited over things like pie and hot cocoa, the way that some children did about a new toy or game.

Once their unpacking was done, Carrie bundled Fi up and donned her own winter coat before leaving the very homey and pretty boarding house. The owners, Arthur and Gwen Hanover, had been welcoming and helpful.

Although only eight, Fi was a determined, fearless child and she liked to do as much as possible on her own. Therefore, she held her crutches in her right hand, hung onto the banister with her left, and hopped down the stairs on her good leg. Carrie walked beside her, ready to catch her if need be.

Once out on the street, they turned left.

"Mommy! Look! Donkeys!" Fi shouted, stopping to point.

Carrie saw a Chinese man in jeans and a wool-lined denim coat walking towards them. A dark brown burrow and a lighter gray one followed him without any lead ropes. The brown one wore a pretty green sweater with a lacey, ruffled collar while the gray one wore a leather vest with a badge on the left shoulder.

As they got closer, the man stopped when he saw the way both women looked at the oddly attired equines. "Hi. I'm Dr. Wu and these are my friends. This one is Sugar," he said, indicating the brown burro. "And this guy here is Basco. I always like to introduce new people to them, so when they see them roaming around by themselves, they won't be scared of them."

Sugar gently nuzzled Fi, urging her to scratch her ears.

"May I, Mommy?" Fi asked.

"Sure," Carrie said. "I'm Carrie Sheehan and this is my daughter, Fiona."

"It's nice to meet you."

Carrie said, "May I ask where your office is located? I'd like to establish services for Fiona."

He smiled. "Well, you'd better do that with my wife since she's the human doctor in town. I'm a veterinarian."

Carrie said, "I'm sorry. I didn't realize, Dr. Wu. Although, it does make sense that a vet would have animals following him around."

"That's ok. My name is Winslow, but most everyone calls me Win."

Fi said, "And you can call me Fi. See my leg?"

"Uh huh," Win said, crouching down. "What happened?"

"I had polio a while ago and my leg got messed up. It doesn't hurt now, it just won't hold me," Fi said.

Win smiled. "I'm glad it doesn't hurt and that you're better. Why don't you come see Erin, that's my wife, tomorrow morning for a checkup? Our building is right down the street.

Carrie looked where he pointed, and she saw a large sign that read

"Echo People & Pet Clinic." Underneath it said, "We cut hair, too." Then she noticed a barber's pole hanging under the sign.

Win chuckled at her confused expression. "Erin's clinic is on one side and mine is on the other. I'm also a barber."

"Goodness, you must be busy," Carrie said.

"Yep. And I'm part owner of a sheep ranch," he said.

"Oh! You're *that* Winslow Wu! I can't believe I didn't realize it," Carrie said. "I've come to marry Gino Terranova and he mentioned you in his letters a few times, since you take care of their livestock. He speaks very highly of you."

"I'm glad to hear it. A mail-order bride, huh? My wife was a mail-order bride, too. It worked out great. We're very happy. We have a three-year-old daughter, Mia," Win said.

Fi giggled as Basco lipped one of her crutches. "You can't eat that, silly."

"Basco, Sugar, sit," Win said, snapping his fingers.

Both burros promptly lowered their backsides to the ground and Carrie and Fi laughed. Win went over to Sugar. "Shake." She gave Win her right front hoof and Basco raised his without being told. Win shook it then said, "Up." The burros sat up in a begging position while the two females clapped.

Several other people clapped, too. They were all used to the town mascots and enjoyed them.

Win gave two sugar cubes to Fi. "Wanna give them their reward?"

"Yes, please."

"Ok. Hold your hand real flat, like this. Then they won't accidentally bite you. It's just the way their teeth are made. They're not mean at all," Win said.

Fi did as directed, giggling when their whiskers tickled her palm. Win had a reason for doing all of this with the child. He was assessing her fine motor skills and coordination, and from what he could see, her upper extremities and her right leg were just fine. She had good balance, too, propping her crutches under her arms as she held out both hands to his pets.

"That was good," he said. "Well, I'll let you ladies get where you're going, but I'll tell Erin that you'll be in tomorrow about nine. See you then."

"All right. Thank you," Carrie said.

"'Bye, Win."

He smiled and went on his way, Sugar following him. Basco stood still, undecided about which to follow. He usually followed Win and Sugar, but he was drawn to the little girl, too. Finally, he trotted after his dam and master, but the little girl didn't completely leave his mind.

The diner was somewhat rundown, but they had good food. As they supped on their vegetable beef soup, bread, and custard cream pie, Carrie looked surreptitiously around at some of the townsfolk. She overheard snippets of conversation, but it was meaningless to her since she didn't know anyone.

A few of the men nodded to her, and she gave them small smiles in return. The diner door opened and several children entered. Carrie noticed that there were two older boys who were Indians. One of the girls with them was also an Indian. There was a blond boy who looked about the same age as the two Indian boys, and a younger girl and boy.

They were a little noisy, laughing and teasing each other as they sat at the counter. Carrie heard a man seated somewhere behind her say, "Filthy Indians!" His voice carried and the schoolkids heard it.

The taller blond boy narrowed his blue eyes at the man and walked past Carrie, right up to the man's table.

"You best be watchin' your mouth, mister," he said. "They have as much right to be here as you do."

"Don't you sass me, boy," the man said. "I'll say anything I damn well please. Besides, what are you gonna do about it?"

The boy said, "I don't think you want to find out. You do know who my pa is, don't you? Let's just say I've learned some things from him and some of my friends. I'm not someone you want to mess with." He walked back to his friends who just smiled at him.

A short, wiry man with graying brown hair that stuck up all over came out of the kitchen. "Well, look at you lot. Back for more of those brownies, huh?"

"Hi, Boss. Yes, sir," one of the Indian boys said. "The ones with the walnuts."

Elias Dexter was called Boss by everyone, and had been as long as anyone could remember. "You're gonna start lookin' like a walnut, Dog Star," he teased. "I think we might have some lying around somewhere. You want the whole pan again?"

Dog Star put some money on the counter. "Yeah. We all went together for them."

"Ok. Be right back," Boss said, returning to the kitchen.

Gino had told Carrie a lot about Echo, including that there was an Indian school near the town. She'd only met a few Indians in Springfield, but she knew that she'd be meeting quite a few of them soon. Gino's brother-in-law, Arrow, was a Cheyenne brave who helped run the school. She was looking forward to meeting his family—that was if Gino didn't end their relationship before it started.

There was a very good possibility that he would, and while she couldn't blame him, she was hoping that the kindness she'd sensed in his letters and had seen during the carriage ride to Echo would cool his anger enough to hear her out.

Boss returned with two pans of brownies. "Here. Take this other one for the other kids, ok? On the house."

Dog Star grinned. "Thanks, Boss."

The others also thanked him before heading out the door again.

"Good riddance," said the complainer.

Carrie had to work hard not to say anything, but Boss glared and pointed at him. "You got a problem with who comes in my place, Burt, you can get out and not show your ugly face in here again. I won't have you talkin' to nobody like that. Got that?"

Burt gave Boss an angry look. "Yeah. Sure."

Boss gave him a parting, warning look and went back into the kitchen.

Carrie felt that it was best for her and Fi to leave before anymore unpleasantness occurred. She paid their bill and they left. Since it was almost dark and it had become colder out, Carrie picked Fi up and walked briskly back to the boarding house to get out of the frigid weather.

She was startled to see Gino come out of the parlor as she hung up their coats.

"Hello, Mr. Terranova," Fi said. "We just had soup and pie and hot cocoa."

He smiled at her bright expression. "Did you? Was it good?"

"Yes."

"I'm glad."

Although he appeared pleasant, Carrie saw his anger near the surface. Swallowing as her meal turned sour in her stomach from nerves, she guided Fi into the parlor and put her up on the sofa.

Gwen came into the room. "Oh, you're back, Carrie. I'm glad you're in out of this weather," the middle-aged woman said.

Carrie smiled. "Yes, it's cold out. I hate to impose, but would you mind watching Fiona for just a little while I speak to Mr. Terranova?"

Gwen said, "I'd be delighted to."

Carrie said to Fi, "You stay here with Mrs. Hanover and I'll be back soon, honey."

"All right, Mommy."

Gino followed Carrie to the kitchen. The blue, high-necked blouse and dark gray wool skirt hinted at slender curves. Sitting down at the table, Carrie sat straight, forcing herself to meet Gino's eyes as he sat across from her.

"I know you're angry with me—"

"Furious."

"Yes. I'm sure. I deceived you because Fi's welfare depends on me finding a husband who can provide for her. I don't care about myself. She's my life and I don't know if I can afford whatever medical care she may need in the future," Carrie said.

Gino's jaw clenched. "I figured that must be the case. So you're hoping that meeting her will tug on my heart strings enough so that I agree to marry you, right?"

Carrie said, "Yes. I'm not normally so conniving, but I'll do anything for Fi, including this."

Gino grudgingly respected her dedication to Fi, but he was still angry and disappointed. "Why did you think you had to hide her from me?"

"Because I've had two men interested in me, but they didn't want to take on a disabled child who might need more medical care than they could pay for," Carrie replied. "I was desperate to secure her future, enough so that I was willing to pull such a terrible deception on you."

"What are you expecting from me, Carrie? I'm hurt because you didn't tell me about her and give me the opportunity to get used to the idea of you already having a kid. You just assumed that I was like those other guys. You used her to get to me and my money. Do you know what that feels like? Like crap!" Gino said.

"I'm sorry, but what if you'd turned me down the way they did? I'd be back at square one with no more prospects. I'm sorry to be so blunt about it, but it's the truth."

Gino snorted. "So *now* you want to be honest. Do you really even know what honesty is?"

Carrie's spine stiffened. "This is the only thing I wasn't honest about. Everything else in my letters was completely true."

"Good to know," he retorted. "I don't know what to say, Carrie. This isn't what I was hoping for. Call me sentimental, but I always wanted to marry for love, not because of my money. If I'd wanted that, I could've married long ago. I'm afraid to introduce you to my family."

"Why?"

"Because I don't want them to get attached to Fiona because right now, I'm not sure if this is gonna work. We all love kids and Fi's a cute girl. It'll be bad enough if it doesn't work out and I'm attached to her. And what if she gets attached to them and then you have to leave? You really didn't think this through very well," Gino said. "I appreciate that you're so protective and willing to take risks for her, but your lack of concern over my feelings or my family's really pi—ticks me off!"

The fire in his eyes and the harshness in his tone both intimidated and excited her, leaving her confused. Her cheeks burned with shame. She hadn't taken his feelings into account, which was very unlike her. She'd been so focused on Fi that she'd been thoughtless.

"You're right. It was cruel of me to not consider how you would feel. I'm so very sorry. I'll abide by whatever you decide. I know I don't deserve it, but I hope you can forgive me. After all, we did like each other's letters well enough to arrange for me to come here," Carrie said.

"I think you liked my money well enough to come here."

"I've already admitted that that was part of the reason I wrote to you, but that wasn't the only reason," she said. "We do have a lot in common in that we're both finance-minded individuals and we enjoy the same kinds of literature. I enjoyed hearing about your family and your business, too."

Gino couldn't deny that. He'd found her intelligence exciting and they'd discussed the stock market and accounting principles. His brothers understood those things to a point, but their talents lie elsewhere. Sal was their chief dealmaker, able to schmooze and keep good relationships with their customers. His oldest brother, Nick, and his mother, Sylvia, had opened a restaurant the previous February, which had taken off right away. Vanna and Lulu had a joint venture; a salon and boutique in the same building, and they were doing well, too.

Alfredo came the closest to Gino's financial knowhow, but even he got lost after a point. Talking to someone who had an excellent grasp on the more intricate fiscal issues was very enjoyable and he'd been looking forward to more such discussions. Looking into her azure blue eyes, he thought they were pretty and her mouth, although slightly wide, was full and soft-looking. Now that he had the chance to observe her a little closer, he found that her understated beauty was very appealing.

His scrutiny was rather unnerving to Carrie because she was certain that he found her lacking. She fidgeted a little bit and cleared her throat.

Her genuine contrition and nervousness brought out Gino's kind, gentle nature, for which he was known. He wasn't used to being so angry and he didn't like it. Sal was the hottest tempered out of the Terranova siblings, his personality was much like Sylvia's. Nick's temper lie somewhere in between the two, while Vanna's sweet temperament endeared her to everyone. Gino was much like Alfredo; cooler-headed and hard to genuinely anger.

In a calmer tone, he said, "I'll think about it tonight and let you know tomorrow."

Encouraged that he hadn't flat out said no to attempting a relationship, Carrie nodded. "That's fine."

Gino rose from the table and said, "Have a good night. I'll see you in the morning."

"You have a pleasant night as well," Carrie said.

Gino said goodbye to Gwen and Fi and left.

Chapter Two

At the Earnest ranch, Gino knocked on the front door of the mansion, still uncertain about coming there. Ronni, Marvin's wife, answered it.

"Hello, Gino. How are you?" she asked.

"Uh, fine, I guess. Sort of," he said.

Ronni said, "Come in out of the cold."

"Thanks," Gino said, stepping into the foyer. "Is Marvin home?"

"Yes. He's in the parlor," she said, leading the way. "Marvin, Gino is here."

Marvin sat in his usual wingback chair by the fire, holding their sleeping son, Isaac, who looked just like his blond-haired, blue-eyed father.

Gino smiled at the sight the father and son made. "He's getting big."

"And bad," Marvin said, smiling. "It's hard to believe he's two already and my sweet Eva will soon be five. They're growing up so fast. That's why we're hoping that lightning will strike twice. Anyway, to what do we owe the pleasure?"

Gino didn't understand his statement about lightning, but he let it go. "Well, speaking of Eva, I was hoping you could give me some advice."

"About Eva?" Ronni asked.

"Well, not about her exactly," Gino said.

Ronni said, "Make yourself comfortable and tell us what you mean."

Gino sat down and explained the situation with Carrie and Fiona.

"I'm so sorry," Ronni said when he was done. "It's a difficult situation to be where she is. I know how hard being a single mother is and losing a dearly loved husband. I was very lucky to have found a man who accepted Eva and loves her as though she's his own."

"She *is* my own. I didn't help create her, but she's mine," Marvin said. "I fell in love with her before I did you, darling."

Ronni smiled. "Why do you think I fell in love with you? You showed me that you had much more heart than people gave you credit for."

"Shh. Don't tell him that. He's my competitor. He'll think I've gone soft," Marvin joked.

Gino chuckled. "Maybe where kids are concerned, but not business. I'm not stupid."

"Well, that remains to be seen," Marvin said, shifting Isaac a little. "What would you like to know, Gino?"

Gino ignored Marvin's barb. "So taking on Eva wasn't hard for you?"

Marvin's blue eyes cooled slightly. "No, it wasn't. My situation was a little different than yours, I suspect. I'm sure all of your apparatus works just fine."

Gino's eyebrows rose. "What do you mean?"

"I could make love, but I couldn't actually father a child. I'd had a botched hernia repair when I was fifteen and until Dr. Avery fixed it, I had no hope of ever getting anyone pregnant. And I wanted a baby very badly."

"So, when Ronni bullied her way into the position as my cook and I met Eva, it was love at first sight. She was the sweetest baby and I spent as much time with her as the warden over here would let me."

Gino looked at Ronni, thinking she would become angry, but Ronni just laughed.

"I didn't know you. It was strange that you wanted to be with her so much. I wasn't going to just let anyone do that," Ronni said.

"And I approved of your protectiveness. Gino, after Ronni and I were married, I still never expected to father a child. We'd talked about adoption and that might not be off the table if I can't father more children. I was thrilled to have a child in my life, whether she be mine biologically or not."

Gino said, "I didn't know that. So that's what you meant about lightning striking twice."

"Precisely. Isaac is our little miracle. We named him that because we had a little birthing party while Ronni was in labor. We told jokes and sang and just acted silly in general because he decided to be stubborn and be breech. We were trying to distract Ronni and keep her calm. Erin got him turned and now here he is. Isaac means 'he laughs', which we thought appropriate given how he came into the world," Marvin said.

Running footsteps sounded on the stairs accompanied by the patter of dog paws. Eva ran into the room along with Barkley, the Earnests' English bulldog.

"Mama, can I have cookies?" Eva asked Ronni, clambering up on her lap.

"You already had cookies," Ronni replied.

Eva said, "I'm hungry."

Marvin smiled. "You're always hungry."

Eva nodded, her curly red hair bouncing. "Yeah."

"Eva, can you say hello to Mr. Terranova?" Marvin asked.

Eva's dark eyes settled on Gino. "Hi, Mr. Tarnova." She gave him a little wave.

Gino smiled. "Hi, Eva. How are you?"

"Hungry," was her reply. She took Ronni's face in her hands and leaned her forehead against her mother's. "Mama, can I please have cookies?"

Ronni laughed. "I'll fix you a snack, but not cookies. Then you have to go to bed or we won't go shopping tomorrow."

Eva frowned a little but said, "Ok. Bread and jam?"

"All right," Ronni said.

Eva slid off her lap and trotted over to Marvin, looking at her brother. "He's seeping good, huh?"

Marvin put an arm around her. "Yes, he is." He pulled her closer and whispered in her ear. Pulling back, he asked, "Will you do that for Daddy?"

Eva smiled. "Yeah. Bye, Mr. Tarnova." She waved at him again and trotted after Ronni who had already gone to the kitchen.

"One, two, three …" Marvin said, grinning.

Ronni came back in the room. "Don't send your daughter to do your dirty work, Marvin. If you want something ask me your—" She broke off when she saw Marvin smiling. Glowering at him, she smacked his arm and stomped off again.

"You can punish me later, Darling," Marvin called after her.

Gino wasn't sure what to make of the exchange, but he understood that Marvin enjoyed baiting his wife. He didn't approve.

Marvin saw his expression. "Gino, Ronni and I have a rather fiery relationship, which we enjoy. And believe you me, I love her more than life itself. After all, it's not every woman who would love me the way she does. We seem to keep getting off the track. Are you concerned about being able to accept Fiona?"

"Well, yeah, but not for the reason you might think. I'm mad that Carrie didn't tell me about her. She didn't trust me enough to tell me. It really bothers me that she didn't give me more of a chance," Gino said.

"May I ask why you're not talking with your family about this?" Marvin asked.

"Fi is so sweet and anyone would fall in love with her. I'm concerned for her. If Carrie did this, what else has she been dishonest about? I don't want to introduce them to my family and have Fi get attached to any of us if I can't get past her deception," Gino explained. "None of them has ever taken on someone else's child."

Marvin nodded. "I can understand that and I think it's nice that you're thinking of Fiona's welfare, but I also think you should give Carrie the benefit of the doubt. I know that one of the reasons Ronni married me was so that Eva would have security, and that doesn't bother me.

"Let's face it; most women don't have the means to easily support themselves and children on their own. Most people pay them less than men, which I think is terrible, and the cost of living has gone up. If Carrie loves Fiona the way that most mothers love their children, there's nothing she won't do to care for her, including deception. The question is whether or not you can soften your heart enough to understand that."

Gino sighed. "I think I'm more sentimental about it than you. I was hoping to fall in love when I got married. I wasn't looking for an arrangement."

"Ah. A true romantic. You might end up falling in love with Carrie. As this little fellow sleeping on my lap proves, anything can happen," Marvin said.

Looking at Isaac, Gino's curiosity got the better of him. "So you couldn't make babies at all?"

"No. I never had to worry about birth control. Ever," Marvin said. He enjoyed Gino's surprised look. As far as Marvin had come, there would always be a perverse part of him that liked shocking people. "I'm no choir boy, Gino. I make no apologies for that."

Gino grinned. "Actually you *are* a choir boy."

Marvin chuckled. "Yes. I'm surprised the church is still standing."

"I can't believe you started a choir and that you roped Nick into joining it," Gino said.

"I have ways of convincing people to do things. Besides, it's good for the town to have a healthy church. I never used to care about such things before Ronni and Eva came into my life. But I do now. People enjoy it when we perform and if that's the only reason they come to church, that's fine with me," Marvin said.

"Do you even believe in God?" Gino asked.

"Yes, but we have a strange relationship. I'm grateful to Him, but we're not chummy. I doubt that I'll ever have the sort of faith Nick does. Or the rest of you, I suppose."

Gino silently agreed that Marvin's viewpoint was very strange. "But you like singing and playing hymns."

"I like performing period. Shadow, too. We also go to the Burgundy House and sing. Shadow and Thad have done a remarkable job in cleaning it up. So much so that he and I are going to buy it."

Gino raised an eyebrow. "The choir director is going to own a house of ill repute?"

"That's right, but as I said, it's been cleaned up and we'll make sure that there's no more prostitution on the premises or we'll kill Kevin," Marvin said.

Marvin suddenly gave off a vibe that made Gino believe the other man was capable of murder. "Well, I wish you good luck with it. I appreciate the advice."

"Good luck to you, too. Please remind Nick about practice on Tuesday."

Gino said, "Ok. I'll see myself out. Thanks again."

"You're welcome," Marvin said as Gino left. "Well, little man, I think you're out for the night," he said, and took his son up to bed.

Chapter Three

Erin finished Fi's examination and said, "Well, you are a very healthy girl."

Fi said, "Except for my leg. Will it get better?"

"Well, I'm not sure, but it might," Erin said. "I know it's hard, but we'll have to wait and see. In the meantime, there are some things we can do to help you get around easier."

Carrie said, "They did some exercises with her once she got better. Is that the sort of thing you mean?"

"Yeah," Erin said. "Keeping all of her muscles strong, especially her leg muscles, is very important. I see some indications of atrophy of the affected leg, but it's not too severe. I'd like to keep it that way."

Carrie said, "Whatever you think is best, that's what we'll do."

Erin smiled. "Actually, Win and I have some ideas about that. Do you ride?"

"Yes," Carrie said.

"Good. I think one of the best ways to keep Fiona's legs strong is for her to ride. She'll have to grip the horse in order to make it go and to balance," Erin said.

"By herself?" Carrie asked. "She'll fall."

"Not if she rides the perfect steed. Follow me," Erin said.

Carrie wondered at her mysterious smile as she helped Fi off the exam table and gave her crutches to her. They trailed Erin back a hallway to a door that opened into a two-bed medical ward. Another door led into Win's side, a combination veterinarian office and barber shop. Carrie was surprised to see Sugar and Basco lying on a couple of mats of some sort.

As soon as the burros saw company, they got up to greet them. Win was cutting a man's hair. "Good morning, ladies," he said.

"Good morning, Win," Carrie said.

"I see Erin brought you to meet her new exercise equipment," he remarked.

Fi asked, "What's that?"

Basco inspected Fi's crutches and then nuzzled her hair a little as a little girl ran over to them. Erin scooped her up, hugging her.

"This is our daughter, Mia and she just turned three. Say hello, Mia," Erin said.

"Hello," Mia said, smiling.

"Hi," Fi said.

Carrie said, "Hello, Mia. What a pretty girl you are. What did you mean about exercise equipment?"

Erin chuckled and put Mia on Basco's back. "Take him around, Mia."

Mia said, "C'mon, Basco. Let's go."

The burro moved away from the women, and Mia guided him on a circuit of the office while they all watched with smiles.

"Faster, Mia," Win said.

Mia tapped her heels to Basco's sides, and Basco broke into a slow trot. Carrie watched in amazement as the toddler guided the burro over to Win, around the office and then into the ward and back again. Mia came back with him and stopped him.

"Sit," she commanded.

Basco sat down and Mia slid from his lap with a giggle. Mia was outgoing and liked making new friends. She went over to Fi and said, "Your turn. C'mon."

"Can I, Mommy?"

Carrie was torn. While she was sure that the doctors wouldn't let any harm come to Fi, her daughter had never ridden a horse by herself. Carrie was worried about her falling off because of her weakened leg. However, if riding could help Fiona, Carrie wanted her to do it.

"All right, but I'll walk with you."

Fi's face lit up and she went over to the burro, who still sat down. "How do I get on?" she asked Mia.

"Like this." Mia simply laid down on Basco. "Up!"

Basco slowly stood again.

"See? Easy," Mia said. "Sit, Basco."

He put his rump back on the floor and Mia slid off again. "C'mon," she said to Fi.

Carrie took Fi's crutches and steadied her until she had a hold of Basco's vest.

Mia stepped forward and took one of Fi's hands. "Grab this." She guided her hand to a loop of leather. "Over there, too."

Fi saw another loop on the other side of the vest and grabbed it. "Now what?" she asked.

Mia whispered in Fi's ear and backed up.

"Up, Basco," Fi said.

Basco turned around to look at Fi in confusion, since she was a new rider to him. Then he rose slowly until he stood erect. Fi's natural instincts made her sit up. She adjusted her seat a little and broke into a huge smile.

"Mommy! Look at me! I did it!" she said.

Tears stung Carrie's eyes at her daughter's happiness. "Yes, you did. Good girl."

Fi turned to Mia. "How do you steer him?"

Mia said, "Tap here to go that way." She pointed to the right. "And tap here to go that way." She motioned to the left.

Fi touched the heel of her good leg against Basco's side and tapped his left shoulder. He obeyed her commands and walked around the office. Carrie walked with them, but after the second time around, Fi said, "I can do it, Mommy. Please let me try."

Carrie nodded, but was loathe to leave them. However, she stood back and watched Basco walk around again. Mia told Sugar to sit and hopped on her back. The adults grinned as they watched the two little girls ride the burros around the office.

In a few minutes, Erin said, "We'll have regular riding lessons and there are some other things we can do, but it's a good place to start."

Carrie said, "I can't thank you enough."

"None needed," Erin said. "It's as good for Sugar and Basco as it is Fiona."

Fi told Basco to sit and he plopped his butt on the floor, allowing her to slide off. Carrie had her put her coat on and thanked the doctors again before leaving. Gino hadn't yet come when they'd left for the clinic, and Carrie didn't want to miss him. She'd asked Gwen and Sofia to tell him where they'd gone in case they weren't back yet.

When they arrived back at the Hanovers', Gino was sitting in the parlor. He stood when he saw them come in the door.

Carrie said, "Good morning. I'm sorry I forgot to tell you about our appointment this morning. I hope you weren't waiting long."

"No, not long. Don't worry about it," he said. "It's good to see you, Fi."

"You, too, Mr. Terranova," she said. "I rode on Basco. It was a lot of fun."

Gino smiled. "You did? He's pretty neat. Sugar, too."

"Yeah. I'm going to ride him to help my legs," Fi said. "I can't wait to do it again."

"Dr. Avery said that it will strengthen her muscles," Carrie said.

"Yeah, it will," Gino said. "You have to be able to grip with your legs when you ride, especially if you're cuttin' cattle and you need to keep your hands free. You'll see. In fact, are you busy today?"

Carrie shook her head. "No. I hadn't planned anything since we just arrived."

Gino said, "Ok. Well, I thought you might like to see our ranch."

She understood from his expression and the tone in his voice that he'd decided to give a relationship with her a chance. "We'd love to," she said, feeling giddy.

Fi nodded. "I want to see all the cows."

"There's enough of them to see, that's for sure," Gino said. "Did you need to do anything before we leave?"

"No," Carrie said.

"All right. I have a buggy out back," he said.

As they walked through the kitchen and left the house, Gino's instinct was to pick Fi up and carry her, but something told him that she wouldn't like that. He noticed that although Carrie walked close to her, she didn't offer to carry Fi. However, he did pick her up to put her in the buggy.

He helped Carrie into it and took the place on the front seat by her. "You all right back there, Fi?"

"Yep."

Gino started out and pointed out the various businesses and so forth to the ladies, answering their questions and telling them more about his friends. Once they left the town behind, the conversation lulled. Carrie grew nervous, not wanting him to find her dull. His good looks drew her eyes and she worked hard not to stare at his handsome profile.

"How are you doing this quarter?" she asked suddenly. "You said that you were expecting an increase in the sales of the chickens that you started raising."

"Well, I'll know better by mid-March, but right now it looks promising. It's a strange situation in a way. Nick buys chickens for the restaurant almost every day from a local chicken farmer. We got to thinkin', why cut into his business when we could just form a partnership? So that's what we've done.

"He already had the set up for chickens and he has the expertise in raising them, which we don't. So, it just made more sense to help him expand his operation and split the profits accordingly. It's working out good so far."

"I'm glad to hear it," Carrie said. "A new venture is exciting and scary, but it sounds as though you have it well in hand."

"So far, so good," Gino said.

Their conversation continued, both of them enjoying exchanging fiscal ideas and discussing the stock market. Carrie had been in the middle of a sentence when they turned up the long drive to the Terranova estate. She trailed off as the house came into view around a bend in the drive.

The red brick, two-story mansion stood proudly against the blue sky overhead. A balcony ran around the second story of the structure. Two red barns stood off to the left and vast pastureland stretched out beyond the horizon. Woods ran behind the house and seemed to also go on for miles. On the right side of the house stood a large greenhouse.

Gino had lived there for so long that he didn't notice how impressive the place was anymore. Seeing the expression of wonder on Carrie's face made him view it through her eyes, and he was proud of their family home. They'd worked hard over the years to build the ranch into its present condition.

"Wow!" Fi said. "It's so pretty!"

"My thoughts exactly," Carrie said. "You said that it was big, but I didn't know you meant a mansion."

"Oh," Gino said. "I guess I forget sometimes that that's the technical name for it. We just call it the house."

"Well, that's some house," Carrie said, a little overwhelmed.

Gino hid a smile at her expression as they pulled up in front of the house and stopped. He helped Carrie and Fi out of the buggy and led the way inside the house.

Taking them into the parlor, Gino said, "Make yourselves comfortable. I'll go get the parents. I'm not sure who all is here right now, but I'll round them up so you can meet them. They've been excited about meeting you. I'll be right back."

Carrie helped Fi up onto the sofa and looked around the beautiful parlor. Although all of the furniture was of excellent quality, it looked well-used and the room had a lived-in feel to it. Some magazines sat on a stand that stood in between two red and gold wingback chairs. Each had ottomans and it looked like feet were often propped upon them. A sewing basket sat on the floor by the other chair.

Various paintings hung on the wall. One of them was a lovely depiction of the Terranova estate and another one showed the inside of an Italian restaurant. Carrie smiled when she realized that it must be Nick and Sylvia's restaurant. She wondered who the artist was as she looked at the beautiful rendering.

Gino returned with his parents and a man, whom Carrie assumed was Sal. They were accompanied by a very pregnant woman and a beautiful redhead. Gino made all of the introductions and Carrie and Fi were warmly greeted.

Sylvia said, "Fiona, you look like a little angel with that beautiful blonde hair."

Fi beamed. "Thank you."

"I put on some coffee, and I'm making some hot cocoa," Sylvia said.

Carrie said, "You don't have to go to any trouble."

Alfredo said, "It's no trouble. We like entertaining and we're glad to have you here. We're big on hospitality. We can't help ourselves."

"Thank you very much," Carrie said.

"Think nothing of it," Sylvia said, leaving the room.

The others sat down, Sal helping Lulu sit in one of the chairs. She sighed and rubbed her large abdomen.

"I can't wait for this baby to come," she said. "I think I'll eat some spicy food tonight and see if that does the trick."

Sal smiled and rubbed her arm. "My poor *bella donna*. It'll all be worth it, just remember that."

Lulu said, "I just love how men always say that when it's not their bodies that have to do all of the work."

Alfredo laughed. "That's just our way of trying to encourage you. I was the same way with Sylvia all four times she was pregnant. Us guys just don't know what to say sometimes. I'll go see if Syl needs any help."

Carrie's stomach ached from nerves as they sat there. Gino's family was very nice, but she was worried that she would embarrass herself or that Fi would misbehave. Alfredo and Sylvia returned with a coffee pot, cups, and a tray of cookies, which they sat on the coffee table. Once the refreshments were served, they sat having a pleasant conversation.

A little while later, an Indian brave entered the parlor. He smiled at their guests.

"Hello. I'm Arrow. You must be Carrie and Fiona," he said, shaking their hands.

Carrie found her voice. "It's nice to meet you. Gino has told me nice things about you."

"He's said the same of you," Arrow said.

"You have pretty hair," Fi said.

Arrow was used to women's fascination with his long, ebony hair and he wasn't offended. "Thank you. So do you. Would you like to trade?"

Fi laughed. "I don't think we can."

Arrow opted to sit on the floor as he often did. He sat close to the coffee table and took a cookie from the tray, popping the whole thing in his mouth. Carrie noted that his family just smiled.

"I put a new bandage on that young heifer's leg," Arrow told them. "It's coming along, but I don't want it to become infected."

"Thanks," Gino said. "She's from one of our best milkers and I have a hunch that she'll yield a lot of milk, too. It would be a shame to lose her."

Carrie said, "That's right. You're Win's apprentice."

Arrow nodded. "Yes. I also help with the Indian school when I'm needed."

As they talked, Fi watched Arrow closely, mesmerized by his dark eyes and winsome smile. Carrie enjoyed the interaction between all of the Terranovas. They were lively and teased each other constantly.

Sal said, "So, Carrie, we're really grateful to you for taking on Gino."

"What do you mean?" she asked.

"Well, most of the time we don't really understand what he's talking about when he gets past a certain point with the books. You'll be able to keep up with him," Sal said.

Gino grinned. "I know it's time to shut up when their eyes glaze over. I can't help it that I got all of the intelligence."

"You did not," Sal said. "Who's the best wheeler-and-dealer, huh?"

Gino said, "Well, I wanted to leave some smarts for you and Vanna, but I think Vanna got it all."

Sal's blue eyes narrowed. "Very funny."

"I thought so," Gino said.

"Ow!" Lulu rubbed her stomach again. "That was uncalled for, young man."

Sal leaned over. "Take it easy on your mama," he said to her belly.

Carrie said, "Fi used to do that to me all the time. Mostly in the middle of the night."

"I did?" Fi asked.

"Yes. You kept me up many nights, but I didn't really mind," Carrie said.

"Well, someday when I'm gonna have a baby, I hope it doesn't keep me up," Fi said.

Sylvia said, "I hope not, either. Sal was the one who did that to me."

Alfredo grunted. "And to me, too. He used to kick me in the back all night long. Even then he was a pain in my backside."

"Hey, why are you all picking on me?" Sal complained. "I was a baby. What did I know?"

Arrow said, "I don't think you've learned much since then, though."

Carrie laughed along with the others.

Sal said, "Actually, I did. I was smart enough to marry Lulu, wasn't I?"

Arrow grinned, "Yes, but that means that she wasn't very smart for marrying you."

"Arrow!" Lulu said. "How could you saaayyyy—ooh!" She put both hands on her stomach and her face turned red.

Sal was on his knees by her chair in an instant. "Lulu, are you ok?"

She nodded as the pain subsided and she panted. "Well, that was unpleasant," she said.

"Are you in labor?" Sal asked.

"I don't think so," Lulu said. "That's the first time that's happened."

Sylvia said, "We'll keep an eye on you, but I had false labor pains more times than I could count with all of you. Don't panic, Sally."

He trusted his mother's judgment, but he was still uneasy as he rose and sat back in his chair again. He kept a hold of Lulu's hand even as he tried to stop the trembling in his own.

"Carrie, Fiona, would either of you like some more to drink?" Sylvia asked.

"No, thank you," Carrie said.

Fiona shook her head.

"All right. I'll just clear these away then," Sylvia said, rising. She gathered the cups and leftover cookies onto the tray and left the room.

Carrie didn't know what to do. On one hand, she was looking forward to spending more time with Gino, but if Lulu was going to have the baby, she didn't want to intrude on a private family time. There was no way to know at this point whether Lulu was in true labor or not, though. She caught Gino's eye with a questioning look.

Gino said, "Why don't I take you back to town?"

Carrie nodded. "Yes. We could stop by the school."

Alfredo said, "You'll like our schoolteacher, Adam. He and his wife, Allie, are friends of ours. She works for Nicky."

"I'm sure we will," Carrie said. "Thank you so much for having us and for the refreshments."

Alfredo stood with everyone except Lulu, who stayed where she was.

Carrie took her hand. "You take care, Lulu. And if you do go into labor, you'll be just fine. I can see that you're a strong woman. I don't know him all that well, but I'd think you'd have to be to be married to Sal."

Lulu looked at her husband, whose eyes had widened, and laughed. "You really *are* smart. You learn quickly."

"Yeah. A little too fast," Sal said. "That's ok. I'm tough. I can take all of you on."

Sylvia came back and said goodbye to Carrie and Fiona. The family waved to them as they got in the buggy and drove away.

Chapter Four

"I'm sorry our visit got cut short," Gino said as they rode along.

Carrie said, "Don't be. I completely understand. I'm very happy for them."

Gino nodded. "Me, too. I'll tell you what; if Lulu doesn't go into labor by suppertime, how about I come back and we could have dinner at the restaurant? You can meet Nick then."

"Are you sure? That's a lot of running back and forth. I'm sure you have other things to do," Carrie said.

Gino said, "I don't mind. I'm pretty caught up with everything for a few days. I purposely planned it that way so that we'd have time to spend together."

His clearing his schedule told her how much her arrival meant to him, and she felt guilty all over again about her dishonesty. She said, "In that case, we'd love to."

"How's that sound to you, Miss Fiona?" Gino asked, turning around to look at her.

Fi had stretched out sound asleep on the buggy seat.

"I think we tired her out," Gino remarked, stopping the buggy. They usually kept blankets in the buggies, so Gino got one and put it over Fiona.

Carrie was touched by his thoughtfulness. "Thank you," she said when he'd sat back down.

"Sure," Gino said. "I don't want her to get cold."

"Kindness seems to run in your family," Carrie remarked. "You look so much like your father."

Gino smiled. "Yeah. Nick and Vanna look just like Mama. Sal looks like Mama, too, except for his blue eyes, but I'm Pop all over again, as Mama likes to say."

"Well, he's a very handsome man," Carrie said.

"So if he's a handsome man and I look like him does that mean you think I am, too?" Gino asked.

Carrie chuckled. "Yes, of course. But you don't need me to tell you that. I'm sure you've had lots of women tell you that."

Gino's brow furrowed. "Not lately. That's why I advertised for a bride. It's taken me a while to find someone I really liked."

"Forgive me, but I find that hard to believe," Carrie said.

"Why? I'm not lyin'."

She smiled. "No, that's not what I meant. You're rugged, handsome, very intelligent, kind and funny. I can't imagine why a woman wouldn't be attracted to someone like that."

"That's what I said," Gino said.

Carrie's eyes widened. "What do you mean?"

"I don't mean to be blunt, but I know I'm not terrible to look at and I think I'm all of those things you just mentioned, but it's nice to hear someone else think them about me for a change."

He looked at her, a twinkle in his eyes that told her he was teasing her. She laughed, and he joined her.

"Oh boy," she said. "Maybe I'm the one who needs to be strong if I'm going to marry you."

Gino grinned. "You'll need to be strong just to deal with my crazy family period. At least you're Catholic. That'll make things easier."

Carrie sobered. "I'm not Catholic."

He glanced sharply at her. "What?"

She dissolved into laughter at his surprised and disappointed expression. "Got you!"

He lightly punched her arm. "Shame on you! Givin' me a heart attack like that! We broke in an Indian and Lulu to our religion. I really didn't want to do it a third time."

Carrie laughed harder. "I can't even imagine what that must have been like."

"You should try convincing an Indian that he can't trade bear meat for your sister's hand in marriage," Gino said.

"Is that a euphemism for something?"

"No, it actually happened," Gino said, recounting the story about the first they'd met Arrow.

Both of their stomachs hurt from laughing by the time he was done. "So he really did kill a grizzly bear?"

"Yeah. It was the damnedest thing I've ever seen. He just couldn't understand what was wrong with his deal. We tease him about it, but he's a good sport. Vanna couldn't be safer, though. He's a force to be reckoned with no matter if he has a weapon or not. And a prankster, too. He got Pop to lose enough weight so that he could wear a breechcloth this past summer."

"He what?"

Gino had to wait for his laughter to subside before saying, "Last summer, Arrow was teasing Pop about getting old and being a little overweight. Pop doesn't like it when Arrow only wears his breechcloth, which is pretty funny to watch. Anyhow, Arrow told him it's just because he's jealous, since he wouldn't look as good in one. So him and Pop made a bet that by August, he'd be in shape enough to wear one."

Carrie asked, "Who won?"

"Pop. He got Arrow good, too. None of us knew it, but Pop kept collectin' hair from our horses' tails when he'd groom them, and he had Lulu make it into a long-haired wig when he had enough. He waited until everyone else was sitting down for breakfast to unveil his native look. Arrow's brother gave him a breechcloth to wear, in exchange for making sure he was able to be there to see the show.

"So, Pop comes into the dining room wearing only this breechcloth and this wig. He scared us at first. It's a good thing Arrow didn't have his knife on him at the time, or Pop wouldn't be here. I've never laughed so hard in all my life, but I gotta tell you, Pop looked good. We must have laughed for fifteen minutes straight and he kept the wig, too. It hangs in their room. Every so often, Sal asks him if he dressed up for Mama lately, which gets him in trouble."

Carrie shook with laughter as she tried to picture Alfredo doing something like that. "I wish I could have seen that, too."

"You just might someday. Who knows? So, you'll have to get used to us because we're loud and rowdy."

"And a lot of fun from the sounds of it," Carrie said.

"Yeah. We do have a lot of fun," he said as they came into town.

When they arrived at the Hanovers', Gino carried Fi upstairs for Carrie. He laid her on a bed and covered her up.

"Is six ok?" he asked her.

"That'll be fine," she said. "I'm looking forward to it, but if you don't come, I'll know that something happened with Lulu."

"Right," Gino nodded. "Ok. I'll see you ladies then."

Carrie said goodbye and sat down with Fiona. She decided that the next day would be soon enough to take Fiona to the school.

"Darlin', it's gonna be fine," Arliss Jackson told his fiancée, Andi Thatcher, as they waited at the train station in Billings for his parents and grandparents to arrive.

"I know I shouldn't be nervous, but I'm afraid they'll hate me," she said. "This is terrible. I've never been so nervous."

He gathered her close. "I promise that they're not gonna hate you."

"Are you sure? I mean, what if they think I'm too religious?"

With a laugh he said, "Honey, you're a pastor. It doesn't get much more religious than that."

He and his brothers had never seen Andi so rattled, and it was endearing. Their lady was normally unflappable and poised, but right then, she was a wreck.

She leaned her head against his shoulder. "I know. You're right." Taking a deep breath, Andi tried to pull herself together. "There. That's better."

Smiling into her brown eyes, Arliss said, "My folks already love you and do you know why?"

She smiled back. "Because I love all of you."

"That's right. No other woman's ever done that before," Arliss said. "So quit your worryin'."

"Oh! There's the train," she said as it appeared in the distance. "Do I look presentable?"

R.J. came forth. "You look enchanting, love," he said in his British accent. "There really isn't any need to worry. Although we do understand how you must feel because we're nervous about meeting your father tomorrow."

"Oh, R.J.," she said, sympathetically. "He'll like you. I've already explained it all to him. I'm so excited that he's going to perform our ceremony."

R.J. chuckled. "We'll have to be on our best behavior, I suppose. You know how hard that'll be for Blake."

"It's just as hard for you and Arliss," she quipped.

He smiled. "Yes. That's true."

They waited for Dennis and Nora Elders to disembark, along with their grandmother, Greta. R.J. spied them and guided Andi towards them.

"Mother!" he called out.

Nora turned and grinned at him. "R.J.!"

Like Andi, Nora, Dennis and Greta were able to keep up with Arliss' personality shifts and knew which of the three was in charge at the moment just by their voice or their expressions. R.J. hugged their mother and kissed her cheek before greeting Dennis.

"Mother, Father, this is Andi, the love of our life."

Dennis grinned at Andi. "Well, our boys said you were beautiful and I guess they weren't lying. It's a pleasure to meet you."

She shook his hand. "Thank you. The pleasure is mine, Dr. Elders."

Nora said, "I'm so jealous of you, Andi. You don't need help getting things down from the cupboard."

Andi laughed at her teasing remark. It was something people often said to the six-foot-tall woman. "It is convenient," she said. "There are times when I wish I wasn't so tall, though."

"We don't," R.J. said. "We're rather fond of those long legs of yours."

"Stop that," Andi said, giggling.

"Very well. Where's Nana?" he asked.

"Right behind you, handsome."

R.J. turned around. "Sneak attack, hmm?" He wrapped his arms around the short, dark-haired woman and picked her up. "It's so good to see you, Nana!"

"Likewise," she said. "I'm glad to see you haven't been shot lately."

He put her down and introduced her to Andi.

Greta said, "Andi, just call me Nana. It's just easier and I'm not formal."

"Oh, all right, Nana," Andi said. "I'm so glad to finally meet you all."

Nora said, "And us, you." Looking at R.J. she asked, "Are your brothers shy today?"

He smiled. "No, I was merely being selfish."

"Well, stop."

"Yes, Mother."

Arliss and Blake came out by turns and greeted their family members. Then they gathered their luggage, loaded it on top of the carriage that Arliss and Andi had brought and took off for the hotel. Once they were settled, they went down to the dining room and found a table far from other diners, so that Arliss didn't have to worry about being overheard as he and his brothers switched back and forth in rapid succession.

Once they'd ordered, Greta asked Andi, "So what made you fall in love with my grandsons?"

Andi didn't blame her for wondering. It wasn't every woman who would fall in love with a man with Multiple Personality Disorder. She understood why their family would be protective of them.

Looking at Arliss, she said, "Because each of them are good men. They're kind, gentlemanly and they make me laugh so much. Not to mention that they're handsome, each in their own way. They treat me like a queen, too. What woman could refuse all of that?"

Dennis liked the way that Andi referred to his sons collectively. It was obvious that she truly appreciated them. She easily conversed with each personality, much the way that he, Nora, and Greta did. He'd never seen such love in Arliss' eyes, either. Yes, their sons had definitely found a love match. Nora and Greta saw it, too, and were very happy for the couple.

As the meal progressed, Dennis grew even more curious about the abilities that Arliss had told him Andi possessed. She wasn't a circus act, however, and he didn't want to offend her by asking for a demonstration, but Greta didn't hesitate.

"Andi, the boys tell us that you have some unusual abilities."

Andi smiled. "And you're wondering if it's true."

Arliss said, "It's true, all right."

"May I have your hand, Greta?" Andi asked.

Greta gave it to her and Andi closed her eyes. She saw a little girl that she knew was Greta and two other little girls running up a path to a cottage. She smiled as they went into it, calling out for their mother. Entering the kitchen, they found her just pulling a loaf of bread from the oven. Andi could smell the delicious aroma.

Eloise. The name came to her and she said, "Your mother was a beautiful woman, Greta. You resemble her very much. Eloise Bingham. You lived in the prettiest little cottage. There are two more little girls with you. One must be your sister. Velma. What a cute girl. I think the other one is just a friend or maybe a cousin. Tabitha." Andi opened her eyes and smiled into Greta's tear-filled eyes. "Your mother made wonderful bread, didn't she?"

Greta smiled and nodded. "People used to buy bread from her because it was so good. Pies and cakes, too. She was a highly skilled baker. Tabitha was our cousin on our father's side. We were so close that she might as well have been our sister." Greta squeezed her hand. "Arliss was right. You're the genuine article. There's no way you could have known all that because I don't believe I ever mentioned Tabitha to the boys."

Blake said, "And we never told her your mother's name. It never came up."

Dennis and Nora were amazed.

"I've never seen anything like that," Dennis said.

"We told you she's something special," Blake said.

Nora smiled at the pride in his voice. "Yes, you did."

Andi blushed as they praised her and Dennis chuckled. "I think we're embarrassing poor Andi," he said, and changed the subject, asking about Marvin and Win, whom all three of Arliss' relatives had previously met.

Andi was grateful to him for taking the focus off her. The rest of the meal was spent filling their guests in on what had been happening with the Indian school and other events around Echo. By the end of the meal, Andi was feeling much calmer. Her men had noticed because in her mind, clear as a bell, she heard R.J. say, "*Did we not tell you all would be well, my pet?*"

She looked at him and narrowed her eyes at him, but he just grinned back at her. His family noticed and realized that some sort of silent communication was occurring. Suddenly R.J. grunted and sobered. Andi smiled sweetly and continued the conversation as they all rose from the table. The others didn't comment, but they noticed that R.J. walked with a very slight limp.

Chapter Five

Josie Taft, Bea Watson, and Sofia Carter, sat in the choir loft while Nick, Marvin, Shadow, and Arthur Hanover argued hotly over a piece of music and who kept messing up the piece. This was nothing new and these arguments could go on for several minutes at a time. The problem was that all four men thought they were right and knew more about music than the others, which made it hard to settle disputes.

Bea tried to intervene, but the men drowned her out.

Just as Marvin accused Arthur, who sang bass, of being flat, someone played a loud, shrill note on a pitch pipe. Everyone clapped their hands over their ears as they looked towards the sanctuary doors. Henley Remington walked, while smiling, to stand by the choir loft.

"It doesn't sound very harmonious for a choir practice," the redhead said, his green eyes sparkling. "I've come to rescue you from your angry insanity."

Marvin frowned. "What are you talking about?"

"Andi asked me to take over as choir director," he said.

The choir laughed, and although he laughed with them, he didn't leave. "Laugh if you like, but I'm not kidding."

Arthur said, "You don't know how to lead a choir."

"Actually, I do, and I know that you need help," Henley said. "Being in a choir isn't about one person being better than another. It's about coming together for one common purpose; making beautiful music together that touches and inspires other people. In order to do that, you have to help each other to perform as well as possible, not tear each other down for making one little mistake.

"Plus, you men are being very rude to our lovely ladies here, so shame on you for that. You're taking up their valuable time with your bickering. Now, if you're ready to make beautiful music, pipe down and listen. If you're not, get out, because, make no mistake, I'm in charge and it's no problem for me to find people who are willing to play on a team instead of acting like jackasses."

Despite the fact that he was only sixteen-years-old and that he'd delivered his lecture while smiling, the choir couldn't deny his authoritative presence. Although he hated being usurped, Marvin was curious to see how the musical prodigy would handle directing them all.

He bowed a little. "Very well, Mr. Remington. I now hand you the baton."

"Thanks, Mr. Earnest. Everyone come down here." He indicated the area between the pews and the altar. "Come on. The first thing you need to do in order to be able to sing well is breathe properly. Too many people don't realize that there's more to singing than just singing."

Shadow said, "Yes, Henley, we know."

"Do you?" Henley asked as he made them stand in a line. "Let's start with you then, Deputy. Show me the correct way to breathe before singing."

Shadow didn't like being put on the spot, and it showed in the angry look he gave Henley.

Although he began sweating a little, Henley knew he couldn't show fear. "Out there you might be the law, but at choir practice, *I'm* the law. Now show me."

Shadow growled but complied.

"Nope." Praying that Shadow wouldn't crush him like a piece of paper,

Henley put his hand on Shadow's abdomen. "When you take a breath, don't lift your shoulders. Your diaphragm should move, but your shoulders should remain almost motionless. Nick you should remember this from choir, but I doubt you've doing it, either."

Shadow sent Nick a cocky smile because he'd gotten in trouble before repeating the exercise. Henley approved that time. "If you think this is silly, listen to the difference it makes when I sing without breathing properly." He sang a few bars of Amazing Grace and to them it sounded very nice. "And now breathing properly." He sang the same selection, but this time, his voice had much better quality behind it. "See? Makes it a lot better, huh?

"Arthur, this is gonna be real important for you because you're the bass and the lower registers don't carry as well as the upper registers. So you're gonna need more power so you can sing louder to balance it out. You're one person against six others and you add the bottom fullness."

Arthur nodded and Henley walked them through several more types of breathing exercises. "Great. Now you're ready to actually sing. What's our song?"

Marvin said, "It's a slightly different rendition of 'Rock of Ages.' Here," he said, handing the sheet music to Henley.

Henley looked at it for all of three seconds and handed it back. "I see what they did. Very nice. Shadow, you're able sing bass, so I'm going to have you sing with Arthur. Nick baritone, and Marvin on tenor. Ladies, you need some help, too, so I'm going to sing alto since Josie and Sofia sing soprano. We don't need the piano yet, though. Using Amazing Grace, we're going to learn how to sing together."

Bea said, "We already know how to sing together."

"I respectfully disagree with you, Bea," Henley said. "You have to listen to each other closely. So we're going to stand in a circle."

"Do we need to build a campfire?" Marvin joked.

Henley grinned. "I don't think Andi would like that." He played a note on the pitch pipe and had them begin. As they sang, he walked around, make adjustments and reminding them to listen to each other. Since his voice had changed after puberty, he now could sing almost any part and he slipped in and out of each register in order to help the rest.

By the time he had them go through the song another time, they were more cohesive and were enjoying themselves. As the last note faded away, they all smiled at each other, proud of what they'd accomplished. Marvin laughed and got down on his knees, bowing to Henley in reverence. The choir laughed at him and Henley bowed back to him.

"Now you'll be able to sing the songs I picked out for Andi and Arliss' wedding next weekend."

Josie asked, "We're singing for her wedding?"

Henley nodded. "Yep. Don't you think that would be a nice surprise and impress her father, Reverend Thatcher? If we have a good choir, it'll make her look good and after all the good she's done for Echo, I think we should repay her a little, don't you?"

Nick said, "You're absolutely right, Henley. She's helped keep me on the wagon. I owe her in a big way. Do you have the song with you?"

"I sure do."

Bea said, "Well, show us and let's get started." She was playing for Andi's wedding, but the idea of surprising her best friend with such a gift excited her greatly.

"Yes, ma'am." Henley retrieved the copies he'd had printed up for them and handed them out. "Ok, Marvin, on the piano you go."

Marvin hurried to the instrument as the rest of the choir went back to the choir box. Henley had brought his fiddle, but he didn't play it. Instead, he used his bow as a conducting baton. They went through the song part by part, guided by a boy with a fiddle bow, brought together by a common goal: performing beautiful music for two people who were good to Echo in various ways and whom they'd come to love and respect.

When Henley stopped practice for the night, he grinned at them. "See what you can accomplish if you just work together? That was fantastic. Josie, don't you think Billy would sound good singing with Nick since he sings baritone? And Bea, doesn't Keith sing bass? I'm going to guilt my sister Lyla into singing with us. She sings soprano. If you know someone who's a decent singer, bring them and I'll turn them into a great singer. I'll see you tomorrow night out at our house, because we don't want Andi to know what we're up to. Six-thirty sharp. Goodnight, folks."

With that, he picked up his fiddle, gave them a jaunty little wave, and exited the church.

Once she'd made sure her powder-blue dress was neat and that her hair looked nice, Carrie gathered her coat and purse and left her room. She was going to wait for Gino downstairs. Their dinner last night had been wonderful. Mama T.'s served scrumptious, mouth-watering dishes, and their servers were attentive and friendly.

Fi had enjoyed the spaghetti, slurping it appreciatively, while Gino and Carrie had laughed at her. He'd introduced them to Nick, who was just as warm and welcoming as the rest of the family. It had been a delightful evening, and she'd been disappointed when it was over. Tonight, Sofia Carter, who now worked full-time as cook and housekeeper for the Hanovers, was watching Fi for Carrie so that she could spend an evening alone with Gino.

He was taking her to Spike's for dancing since he'd found out that Josie, Billy, and Henley were going to play that night. It was always entertaining when Henley performed, because he usually changed instruments frequently, since there was virtually no instrument he couldn't play or learn how to play. Even though he was only sixteen, Billy had assured his parents that he would keep him safe. Spike paid them each a little something, and they usually made out well in tips, too.

The thought of being alone with Gino both daunted and excited Carrie. Fi was lively, which helped keep the conversation going. She worried that things would be quiet and awkward between them without her there. It had been two years since her husband had passed and she hadn't been courted since then, so she was out of practice with relating to a man one-on-one in a romantic sense.

Just as she was coming downstairs, the front door opened and Gino stepped into the foyer. He caught sight of her and smiled. Her heart beat a little harder as she saw how handsome he looked in jeans, a black wool coat and a black cowboy hat. He'd told her to wear something a little less formal since they were going to a saloon.

"Well, don't you look pretty?" he remarked. "That's a nice color on you."

She thought that it was an unusual thing for a man to say. "Thank you," she said, smiling as she came down the stairs.

"I can't help noticing that kind of stuff now since Vanna and Lulu are always talking about fashion. I've picked up some things," Gino said. He'd seen her surprised expression.

"There's nothing wrong with a man appreciating fashion."

"I'm glad you think so," he said. "Are you ready?"

"Yes."

Gino took her coat from her and helped her into it. She smelled like some sort of flower, but he couldn't quite identify the scent. It reminded him of a spring meadow, and it was enticing on her. She turned around, and as their gazes caught and held, she thought she saw a spark of attraction in them. Could it really be that he found her pretty? She hoped so. It would be awful if the attraction was one-sided, and she *was* attracted to him. She didn't understand how any woman couldn't be.

"Ok. After you, ma'am," he said.

She smiled and went out ahead of him. Once they were in the buggy, Gino said, "I think Sal's gonna lose his mind if Lulu doesn't have that baby pretty soon. She keeps getting those pains every so often, and I don't know how much more his nerves can take."

Carrie chuckled. "I can just imagine. He's excitable to begin with, but something like this would be so much worse for him."

Gino said, "He's constantly watching her, and I don't think he's sleeping much judging by how much he's yawning. And poor Lulu is so uncomfortable."

They continued talking about the Terranova couple, what he'd been doing that day and soon they were at Spike's. Entering the establishment,

Carrie saw that it was medium in size and had a quieter atmosphere than other saloons, not that she'd been in many. Her husband had taken her to an Irish pub in Springfield every so often.

Gino introduced her to Spike, who was in his early seventies. He was a handsome older man with gray hair and blue eyes. He was gruff yet friendly as he greeted her.

"It's a pleasure to meet you, Mrs. Sheehan. You'll have to get used to a lot of noise if you're gonna be around his family."

"Likewise. I think I'll get along just fine. My late husband had a large, Irish family, so I'm used to that sort of thing," she said.

"Well, that's good then," Spike said. "It'll make it easier on you."

Gino ordered them a couple of beers and they sat down at an empty table. No sooner had their bottoms hit their chairs than a big, blond man sat down with them.

He stuck out his hand to Carrie. "Allow me to introduce myself to ya, Mrs. Sheehan," he said. "I'm Lucky Quinn and it's a pleasure to meet ya."

His laughing, gray eyes, and mischievous smile made her feel at ease with him right away. Her husband had had much the same effect on people. "Well, now, 'tis always a pleasure to meet such a fine lad as yerself," she said, mimicking his brogue perfectly.

Lucky's robust laugh rang out as they shook hands. "If I didn't know any better, I'd swear ya were from home."

"Well, I did spend eight years around a big Irish family. I was bound to learn a few things," she said.

"I'd say ya learned them well. Oh, here comes my wife. Leah, this is Carrie Sheehan, Gino's lass," he said as a beautiful, dark-haired woman with brown eyes joined them.

Leah, who was deaf, didn't always like speaking out loud, because she thought she sounded funny, but since neither Gino nor Carrie signed, she said, "Hello. It's nice to meet you."

The two women shook hands and Leah sat down with them. Lucky was never out of stories or things to talk about and their conversation flowed easily as he and Leah told them about their sheep farm and Leah's cobbler shop. An Indian snuck up behind Lucky, got him in a choke hold, and almost drug him off the chair.

They laughingly tussled and wound up on the floor while the other three at the table laughed at them. When they quit their playing around, Lucky introduced Billy Two Moons to Carrie.

"He's one of my best friends. More like a brother and a more talented artist ye'll never see," he said.

Carrie asked, "Did you do the painting of the Terranovas' farm that's in their parlor?"

Billy was surprised. "Yeah. I did it for them last autumn."

"I agree with Lucky, then. It's lovely. You have an excellent eye and incredible talent," Carrie said.

Billy smiled bashfully. "Thanks. I'm glad you like it."

"Billy just became a father again in November," Lucky told them.

Carrie said, "Congratulations! Boy or girl?"

"A little girl. She looks just like Nina, my wife. Blonde hair, green eyes. We named her Michelina, after my ma's mother, and we call her Micki. She's beautiful," Billy said proudly.

Carrie said, "I'm sure she is."

Lucky nudged Billy's arm. "Show 'em yer picture."

Billy pulled a picture from his wallet and handed it to Carrie. "Our boy, Tommy, is three now. We just had that taken in January."

The little boy had dark hair like Billy and his smile. Even though it was a black and white photo, it looked as though his eyes might be a lighter color. He sat on a young, blonde woman's lap, holding his baby sister in his.

"What a beautiful family, Billy. They're adorable and you certainly have a beautiful wife," Carrie said, handing the picture to Gino.

"Thanks," Billy said. "I'm a lucky man. Oh, it looks like Josie and Henley are waiting on me. I hope you have a good time tonight."

"I'm sure we will," she said.

Billy took his picture back and went to get ready to play. Soon, the music began, and couples took to the dancing area that had been cleared of tables. Gino insisted on dancing, even though Carrie resisted at first.

"I'm rusty," she said.

"Well, the best way to get the rust off is to get back at it again," he said. "C'mon. It's not about how well you dance, it's about havin' a good time. If you trip, I'll say it was my fault, ok?"

She couldn't refuse him and she put her hand in his, noting the callouses on his palm. He led her to the dance floor and took her in his arms. It had been so long since a man had held her, that Carrie was stiff with nerves. Gino wondered at her anxiety.

He leaned closer to her. "Hey, it's ok. Just relax. We're just here to have fun."

"I'm not sure I know how to have fun anymore," she said. "I haven't done anything like this since Aidan passed."

"Well, as you can tell, our family likes to have fun, so we'll have to get you back into practice with that, too," Gino said, smiling. "Close your eyes and just listen to the music. We don't have to talk. Just listen to the music and move with me. Let it relax you."

Carrie did as he suggested and shut her eyes, letting him lead her as she listened to the song the trio was playing. She smiled and began humming along, her body relaxing and her steps becoming more fluid.

As she did, Gino watched her face, thinking that she was very pretty. He couldn't sing worth anything, but he had an ear for music. He knew a good singer when he heard one, and Carrie's slightly throaty alto was very pleasant to his ear.

As they danced, he shifted her slightly closer to him and he discovered something; she wore her clothing a little too big. She wasn't as slender as she appeared to be. He slid his hand slightly down her back and felt that she was a little curvier then he'd thought. Why would she hide her beauty like that?

When the song was almost over, she opened her eyes to find Gino smiling at her. She laughed and blushed. "I think your idea worked very well. It's hard for me not to sing along."

"You have a very pretty voice. I enjoyed hearing it," Gino said. "You should sing with Sal and Nick sometime. Nick sings baritone and Sal sings tenor. I don't sing or play anything. I just dance."

"And you do it very well," she said. "You kept me upright while I had my eyes closed, so I'd say you have talent."

Gino said, "Thanks. Having fun now?"

Carrie gave him a flirtatious look, something she hadn't done with a man in a couple of years. "Why, yes, Mr. Terranova, I am."

The way her eyes trailed down over him made his blood pressure rise. Until that moment, he hadn't noticed that her glasses seemed to emphasize her cornflower-blue eyes, instead of detracting from them.

His smile was slightly lopsided. "I'm glad to hear it. The fun's only beginning, though, so hold on."

She laughed when he spun her around and changed tempo when the next song was a faster number. People often traded partners, and it was a fun way to meet and get to know everyone a little. There was a lot of teasing without any stilted conversation.

The musicians spelled each other here and there so they could dance. Josie and Billy forced Henley out onto the dance floor, where he was snapped up by one woman or another. He was tall for his age, but he was graceful despite his long limbs.

By the time the evening was over, Carrie was slightly hoarse from laughing and talking so much. When they left, the cold air felt refreshing after all of the activity.

"I needed that," Carrie said as they rode back to town. "Thank you for such a fun time."

"You're welcome. I had a lot of fun, too. You're a great dancer and easy on the eyes, too," Gino said.

His compliment made her feel good. "Well, I don't know about that. I know I'm probably not what you were expecting."

Gino said, "I didn't form any expectations. What would be the point? I'm sure your husband told you how beautiful you are. Why do you downplay how attractive you are?"

Carrie's mouth opened and closed. He'd found her out, but she didn't know how. "Do you mean my glasses?"

"No. I like your glasses."

"You do? Why?"

Gino said, "Your eyes are pretty enough on their own, but your glasses draw even more attention to them."

She blew out a breath. "Well, you'll be disappointed to know that they're not real. They're costume glasses."

Gino pulled the horse to a stop. "What? They're fake? Why would you wear fake glasses?"

Carrie took them off, saying, "After Aidan died, I was in mourning, but I still had men approach me. I got tired of their attentions, so I started wearing my clothes loser and added glasses. You know how people are about glasses. They think you're weak or unhealthy if you wear them, which is stupid.

"Then Fiona became ill, and I didn't want to be bothered then, either. So I continued dressing like this. Then when I met you, I was so disappointed because you're so handsome."

Gino shook his head slightly. "I don't understand. I'm glad you think I am, but why is that a disappointment?"

"Because I'm sure you were expecting a beautiful woman, and I look rather dowdy."

Gino could tell that she wasn't fishing for compliments. "Carrie, I was expecting a beautiful woman and I got one. Even dressing like that and wearing glasses can't hide how pretty you are. I'm not gonna tell you how to dress, but you don't have to worry about unwanted attentions from other men. I'll make anyone who bothers you very sorry."

She liked his protectiveness. "Thank you for both the compliment and looking out for me."

"You're welcome," he said, starting the horse out again. He glanced at her and said, "You look different without your glasses."

"Better?"

"No, just different," Gino said. "Doesn't it bother you to wear them since you don't need them?"

"No. I got so used to them, that it feels strange not to wear them," she said.

"Go ahead and put them back on."

"Put them back on?"

"Yeah."

His odd expression made her curious. "Why do you want me to?"

Gino shrugged bashfully. "Because they're sort of alluring."

"My glasses are alluring?"

Gino felt himself blush and wished he hadn't said anything. *You'd think you'd never been with a woman, Gino. That's certainly not the case. I'm not like Sal, but I'm no saint, either.* He had to answer her. "Yes. They are."

She almost giggled at his terse response. His discomfort was endearing. She took out her glasses and looked at them. It had never occurred to her that a man would find them appealing. She decided to test him.

"So, if I just slip them on like this, does that look alluring?"

His blood warmed as she slowly put them on while giving him a sidelong glance. Desire made his stomach clench and he almost stopped the buggy to kiss her. "Yeah, it does."

The naked hunger in his eyes was both alarming and thrilling to her. She had nothing to fear, however, because he never made a move towards her. She reined in her disappointment, hiding it behind a smile.

"I'll keep that in mind," she said, taking them off again and tucking them into her purse.

He chuckled, and returned his attention to the road ahead, using the distraction to combat his reaction to her. When they reached the Hanovers', he walked her to the door.

"Thank you again for such a wonderful time," she said.

"You're welcome." They looked into each other's eyes for a few moments. "Oh, the hell with it," he said, cupping her face and brushing his lips against hers.

Carrie froze at the contact and shuddered slightly. Gino felt it and pulled back, thinking that he'd startled her. "I'm sorry. I shouldn't have done that."

"It's all right. It was just unexpected, that's all," she said. "I didn't know you'd want to kiss me."

"Why wouldn't I? I just told you how beautiful you are and how much those glasses drive me crazy. So doesn't it follow that I'd want to kiss you, especially after you teased me with them?"

She arched an eyebrow at him. "Why are you getting angry?"

"I'm not," Gino said. "I'm just saying that it's reasonable after a nice evening and how beautiful you are that I'd want to kiss you."

"Well, I'm sorry if I was being dense," she said, irritated.

He laughed. "I've never argued about kissing a woman before. At least you're not boring."

She smiled and reached into her purse, pulling her glasses out.

Gino sobered. What the heck was it about those glasses? "C'mon, Carrie. You're killin' me with those things."

Emboldened by the way his eyes smoldered, she slid them on, giving him a sultry look.

She wasn't playing fair, so he decided that he wouldn't, either. "*La tua bellezza è simile a quello di un fiore del deserto in piena fioritura; selvatica e accattivante,*" he said.

She'd forgotten that he spoke Italian. A shiver ran through her as he spoke the romantic language in a low, seductive tone, his eyes never leaving hers. "Wh-what does that mean?"

"I said, 'Your beauty is like that of a desert flower in full bloom, wild and captivating.'" Gino told her.

Her lips parted as she gasped a little, and it was too much for Gino. He pulled her to him, pressing his mouth firmly to hers as need drowned out all else. The sweet softness of her mouth was intoxicating and he felt like he'd never get enough. He wasn't alone in that. Carrie wrapped her arms around his neck, holding him tightly as she kissed him back.

He growled against her lips and it brought reality crashing down on her. Much as she didn't want to, she pushed against his chest to stop him. He made a sound of protest, which made her giggle and push harder.

Gino released her with a laugh. "Ok, I can take a hint. Would it be all right if I pick you and Fi up around four tomorrow to come for dinner?"

"That'll be just fine. I look forward to it. I'll make sure to wear my glasses."

"And I'll speak a lot of Italian," he said, grinning.

"Goodnight, Gino."

He kissed her cheek. "*Buonanotte, la mia deserto fiore.* Goodnight, my desert flower."

She waited until he'd gotten in the buggy and started out to go inside. She smiled the whole way up the stairs. Going to their room, she opened the door and saw Sofia reading by lamplight, while Fi was sleeping in her bed.

Sofia smiled at her and whispered, "Did you have a nice time?"

Carrie nodded. "Yes. I haven't had that much fun in a long time. I met Lucky and Leah. They're so much fun. Everyone is. Billy, Josie, and Henley are very talented."

Sofia said, "I'm so glad. Everyone needs to get out like that now and again."

"Thank you so much for watching Fi for me," Carrie said. "Was she any trouble?"

"Not at all. She's such a sweet child," Sofia said.

"Thank you."

They said goodnight, and Sofia left. As she readied herself for bed, Carrie hummed under her breath, thinking about her evening with a charismatic, Italian man who made her weak in the knees.

Chapter Six

"I'm sorry to be so confused, but which one are you marrying?" Reverend Levi Thatcher asked his daughter, as they sat in her hotel room the morning after he'd arrived in Billings.

Andi wanted desperately to make him understand, but she wasn't sure if she could. "Dad, Arliss is what you would call the main personality, so legally I would be marrying him. It'll be his name on the marriage certificate with mine. But, I'll be marrying all three of them. They're the same, yet not. The three make a whole. It's the disorder Arliss has, and it's the only way I can explain it to you. You'll understand once you're around them more."

Levi frowned, "Why do you refer to him as 'them'? He's only one man, regardless of these personalities. I'm not trying to be difficult, Andi. I can see how much you love him, but I'm just not sure he's right for you. He's a spy for Pete's sake! How can you count on him, when he's never around or might not come back at all? That already happened. You thought he was dead and you were heartbroken."

Her father was just as kind as Andi under normal circumstances, but this was his little girl and he wanted to make sure she was going to be safe and well taken care of. Andi understood that her choice in a mate was unusual in many ways, but her heart belonged to her men.

"Dad, Arliss will always do whatever is necessary to come home to me. Their work is very important to the safety of our country. I'm willing to stand by them and help them in any way I can. I love them and I'm so proud of them."

Levi rubbed his eyes. "You're doing it again."

"And I'm going to keep doing it, Dad. Just take a little time to get to know each of them and then you'll understand. Arliss and his brothers are very nervous about this. It's important to them that you approve. Please give them a chance. I know you'll grow to like them," Andi pleaded.

Levi had never been able to deny Andi much. "All right. He seems very nice, but I've just never come across anything like this before."

Andi chuckled. "Me, neither, but they make me so happy and they all treat me so well. They're so thoughtful and bring me little treats when I'm working. R.J. brings me lunch a lot."

"Which one is he?" Levi asked.

"The British one," Andi said.

"R.J. is the British one," he repeated. "Arliss is the main one, R.J. is the British one, and who's the third one?"

"Blake. He's a little rough around the edges, but also sweet in his own way," Andi said.

"Ok. Let me see if I have this right. Arliss is the main one, R.J. is British, and Blake is sort of gruff," Levi said.

"Perfect!" Andi said.

"Right now, but I'm not sure if I'll remember it," Levi said. "I'll do my best."

"That's all I can ask," she said. "Let's go down to breakfast. I'm hungry, and we don't want to be late leaving."

"Right," Levi said.

As he followed his daughter out of the room, he thought, *he's not the only one who's nervous.*

Arliss sat in the dining room with his parents and Greta as they waited on Andi and Levi. Meeting her father hadn't gone completely smooth. He could tell that the reverend didn't wholeheartedly approve, and that he wasn't comfortable around him and his brothers. Therefore, he hadn't let them out at all once they'd each been introduced to Levi.

It reminded him of when he was a teenager and people didn't understand about his condition. It had been embarrassing when people looked at him strangely, and he knew that some people had whispered about him behind his back. After being rebuffed by kids his age, he'd stopped letting R.J. and Blake come out except around their parents, his sister and a couple of friends he trusted.

Andi had tried to reassure him last night when they'd been saying goodnight, but for once, her assurances hadn't comforted him. He was afraid of embarrassing her, and it was a hard fear to overcome, especially because he wanted his future father-in-law to have a favorable opinion of him. Arliss knew that his occupation was another thing that bothered Levi, and he understood why.

"Arliss?"

He looked at Nora. "Huh? Were you talking to me?"

She smiled at him. "Yes. I know you're worried, but you needn't be. Levi will come around. He just needs some time to get used to you all. There aren't very many people who've come into contact with someone as unique as you. Look how much research your father had to do to find information on the condition? There aren't a lot of documented cases. Have some patience with him."

"Listen to your mother, boys. She's a wise woman," Dennis said. "Don't coop the others up, Arliss. I know you have a tendency to do that. He'll never understand if he never associates with your brothers."

Arliss sighed. "All right. I'll try."

Greta patted his arm. "That's our boy."

Andi and Levi entered the dining room and Arliss smiled and waved at them. He stood up when they got close to their table, kissing Andi's cheek and holding her chair for her.

"Good morning, Rev. Thatcher," he said. "Did you sleep well?"

Levi sat down, smiling at him. "Yes, thank you."

"Good," Arliss said. "How about you, darlin'?"

His warm gaze told her how pretty he thought she looked. "Very well," Andi said. "How is everyone?"

As they finished exchanging pleasantries, their waiter came for their order. When he left, Levi looked at Arliss. He'd decided to handle the situation with humor and hopefully break the tension. He'd noticed the uncomfortable set of Arliss' shoulders and the uncertainty in his eyes.

"Arliss, I have a question for you and your brothers," he said.

Arliss became even more on edge. "Ok. Shoot."

"Since there are three of you, do you eat for three?" Levi asked, smiling. "And if so, where do you put it all?"

Arliss was surprised by his joke and laughed along with the others. "You'd think so, wouldn't you? Do you know, you're the first person who's asked us that? The answer is no, but we do all like different foods. I can't cook to save my life, but R.J. is a great cook. Blake likes to cook breakfast, but that's it."

Levi sipped his coffee. "So each of you has his own abilities along with personality?"

"That's right. I play fiddle, I make friends real easy, and I'm a good carpenter. I also pick pockets and locks. R.J. is a card sharp and an assassin, and Blake doesn't feel pain at all, which comes in handy when we get shot or stabbed or something. He's pure muscle power. Combine us all, and you have a very effective and lethal government operative," Arliss said.

Levi had choked a little on the assassin remark, but recovered. Andi hadn't hidden anything from him about Arliss or his line of work, but hearing it from the man himself was a different story. "I see. But you can't divulge who you work for exactly, is that correct?"

"Quite right, Levi," R.J. said. "Not even our parents or Nana know exactly who we're working for at any given time. Andi does, but they don't."

Levi looked at Andi. "You do? He tells you?"

She nodded. "Yes, but not out loud."

He was familiar with Andi's abilities and he didn't doubt what she said. "So you can communicate with them in your minds?"

R.J. said, "Yes. She's able to come to our garden. You see, it's the place where my brothers and I can meet and converse together without anyone hearing us. Andi is able to reach us there. It works long distance, as well. Therefore, while I'm away, we can still keep in touch and let her know what's going on.

"She's actually helped on several of our jobs with some very beneficial insights. It's almost as though she's right there with us. You can't imagine how good it feels to be able to tell someone everything when you work in the sort of field we do. It's a tremendous benefit."

Levi looked at R.J.'s family. "So you never have any idea what he—they're up to?"

Dennis chuckled, "Not completely. I only know whenever they come to be patched up, and usually Blake shows up first when that happens since he can't feel pain. It makes treating them easier."

Andi felt Blake come forth before she noticed the shift.

"Yeah. You could stab my hand with your knife and I'd never feel it," he said. "They would once I fell back, but as long as I'm in control, I can keep going for a long time before my body runs out of steam."

Greta pointed at him. "That might be, Blakey, but we're not going to try that again, are we?"

Blake, who was usually so tough, meekly said, "No, ma'am."

Levi didn't ask about that right then, since it seemed to be a sore subject. Instead, he asked questions and Arliss and his brothers took turns answering him. As they did, he began to see what Andi meant about each of them being so unique. He couldn't see the subtle shift in them the way she and his family could, but he learned their voices.

It thrilled Andi to see them interacting so positively, and she prayed that it continued. Once they were through with the meal, they loaded their belongings on top of the carriages that Arliss and Andi had driven from Echo to accommodate all the people and luggage. Although, they would've preferred to drive together, they'd had to use separate conveyances.

While Levi was a little concerned about Andi's safety in driving alone, he knew that his strong daughter was more than capable of defending herself. Plus, with Arliss right behind her, she'd been more than safe. Greta surprised everyone by wanting to take a turn at driving as they made their way to Dickensville that day. She figured it would give Andi a chance to visit more with Levi and to warm up.

Dennis also took a turn so that Arliss could do the same. He, too, was relieved that Levi had warmed up to his boys. It had been horrible watching Arliss be ridiculed growing up, and Dennis had intervened whenever he was present, fiercely protecting the three of them.

By the time they arrived in Dickensville, darkness was falling, and they were exhausted. They unloaded again and took the teams to the livery stable before eating and going to bed.

As tired as she was, Andi couldn't sleep. Something occurred to her that she'd never thought about before. Could she wake Arliss up by going to the garden? She hadn't tried it before. She knew he wouldn't get angry at her if it did work, so she decided to attempt it.

Closing her eyes, she floated through the sea of blood that was ever present around him, and hoisted herself up over the wall of the garden. She dropped to the ground and looked around with a smile. R.J. liked to change the appearance of the garden from time to time and he'd turned it into a magical place filled with sparkling snow.

Walking down the path a little, she saw a fire burning off to the right, and headed for it. Holding her hands out to the fire, she could actually feel its warmth.

"Arliss? R.J.? Blake?" she called loudly.

Across the hall, Arliss stirred in his sleep, but he didn't quite awaken.

Andi called out to them louder, and her beautiful face rose in Arliss' consciousness. He heard her voice and followed it to the garden, not realizing that he was asleep.

Andi felt hands settle on her shoulders and recognized R.J.'s touch. Turning around, she smiled at him. "It worked."

"What did?" he asked.

"Coming to the garden while you're sleeping," she said.

"Are we?" he asked. "Oh, yes. I guess we are."

Andi then noticed that he was dressed in only his underwear. "Where are your clothes?"

R.J. laughed. "Well, since we're sleeping, I guess you're seeing what we're sleeping in. This is what we wear."

"But you're only wearing the bottoms," she said, trying not to enjoy the sight of his bare upper body too much.

"They're too warm. We tend to get hot while we sleep. Usually by morning, we don't have any covers on us," R.J. said. He saw desire in her eyes. "Don't look at me like that, love. I can't guarantee how much control we have in this dream state. I guess that's what you'd call it."

"I wish it was Saturday," Andi said, longing to touch him.

"So do we."

Her eyes traveled over his sleep-mussed brown hair and blue eyes, chiseled jaw, and broad shoulders. He only stood two inches taller than her, so she didn't have to look up much to look into his eyes, but he was wider than her, with muscular arms and a well-defined torso.

R.J. tipped her chin up and touched his lips to hers, relishing their softness. He was surprised that they could feel it. They'd never tried kissing in the garden before. Of course, she'd never come to them in their sleep before, either. Putting his arms around her, he deepened the kiss.

Andi loved the way all of her men kissed. R.J. was sensual and thorough about it, drawing her in, and igniting her passion for him. Arliss was fun and exciting, and Blake was demanding yet tender. They could also combine and kiss her all at once, but they usually refrained from it, because she became overwhelmed with desire and couldn't think clearly.

Her men had never passed a certain point with her, out of respect for who and what she was, and she loved them for it. Slowly, she broke away from R.J. and leaned her head on his shoulder. "I love you."

He kissed her hair. "We love you. Is it wrong to make love to someone in a dream if they're your intended?"

She looked up at him, tempted to say no. "Yes. Well, I don't know. If it's a dream you don't normally have any control over that. But I'm awake, so yes, it would be wrong for us to. I'd better go before I can't resist temptation."

He gave her a wicked smile. "All right. But if you change your mind, you know where to find us."

He kissed her and sent her on her way. She let herself be pulled back through the sea of blood and into her body. Opening her eyes, she said, "Saturday can't come soon enough."

Chapter Seven

Gino moaned when someone shook him. "What?" he asked, his voice muffled by the pillow.

"Gino, c'mon. Get up. Lulu's having the baby."

Rolling over, Gino recognized his mother. "What time is it, Mama?"

"A little after three," she said.

The excitement in her eyes made Gino smile. "Ready to become a grandma again?"

"More than ready. C'mon. We have coffee on. Nicky went to get Erin."

Gino threw his covers aside and sat up. "And we're sure that it's for real this time?"

Sylvia chuckled. "Well, her water broke, so I'd say so."

Gino grinned as he stood up. "How's Sal holdin' up?"

"Well, I think pretty good under the circumstances. He's worried, but mainly excited. Lulu's scared, but she's ready for this baby," Sylvia replied.

After putting on a robe and slippers, Gino followed his mother downstairs and into the kitchen. Alfredo sat at the table drinking coffee.

"Great hair, Gino," he said, smiling.

Gino said, "I didn't bother combing it. I figure that baby's comin' no matter what I look like." He poured some coffee and sat down with Alfredo.

"So you had a nice time last night?" Sylvia asked.

"Yeah. We danced up a storm," Gino answered. "Carrie's a good dancer."

Arrow came into the kitchen. "Is she a good kisser?"

Sylvia swatted at him, but he scooted out of her reach. "You stop causin' trouble!" she admonished him as he laughed.

"What's wrong with asking that?" His eyes danced with mischief.

"You know exactly why. That's private," Sylvia said.

A smiled tugged at Alfredo's mouth. "Is she?"

"Al!" Sylvia objected.

Gino laughed. "You guys better behave or Mama is gonna kill you." He had no intention of answering their question.

The kitchen door opened, and Nick came in, his face tense. "Neither Erin nor Win could come. They're doin' an emergency surgery. Andi's not back in town yet."

"It'll be fine," Arrow said. They all gave him dubious looks. "Women have been having babies without doctors with college degrees since time began."

Sylvia said, "I don't know how to deliver a baby, do any of you?"

The other three shook their heads.

Arrow said, "Maura and I will deliver it."

Alfredo said, "You will? Have you ever delivered one before?"

"Yes, when I was training to be a medicine man. Maura has acted as a midwife before, too. I'm sure that between the two of us we can handle it," Arrow said.

The room was quiet for a few moments and then Sylvia said, "Well, what choice do we have?"

Arrow gave her a wry smile. "I appreciate all of your confidence in us."

Alfredo said, "We're sorry, Arrow. It's just that we lost one baby in this family, and we don't want to lose another."

Nick's first wife and their son had drowned when their ship sank on the way to Japan. Their loss had devastated the family, but Nick had been utterly crushed and hadn't dealt with it well. He'd begun to rely on alcohol, and his dependence on it had worsened until he'd become an alcoholic.

For a long time, he'd been able to keep his addiction a secret, but then Maura had come along and with her and Sal's help, he'd been able to reach out to his family. They'd been upset at first, but had rallied around him, offering their love and support. Nick was now strong enough to handle alcohol when he was cooking, but he hadn't yet tested himself by being around others who were enjoying an alcoholic beverage. His family refused to drink in his presence.

"I understand," Arrow said. "I will go prepare. Please put water on to boil."

Nick and Sylvia immediately complied, praying for the safety of mother and child.

Lulu sat up in their bed, leaning against Sal, who sat next to her. She'd just had a particularly hard contraction and was resting. He wiped her brow and kissed her head.

"That's right, *bella donna*. Just relax. I'm right here," he said.

"Are you excited?" she asked.

"Am I excited? Of course, I'm excited. How could I not be? I'm gonna be a father soon," Sal said.

Lulu raised her green eyes to meet his blue ones. "Are you sure? I know before your parents made you find someone to marry, you weren't even thinking of having a wife and family."

"All of that's in the past," Sal said. "You how much I love you and I love our baby, too. I couldn't be happier. There's nothing to worry about." He gave her a reassuring squeeze.

A soft knock sounded on the door, and Maura and Arrow entered their two-room suite.

Maura smiled at them. "How are you doing, Lulu?"

"I'm all right," Lulu said.

"Good. Erin and Win can't come because they're in surgery. Andi isn't back yet," the pretty redhead said.

Sal grew alarmed. "Who's gonna deliver our baby?"

Arrow said, "Maura and I will. We both have experience with delivering babies. All will be well."

Maura nodded. "I've been a midwife many times and Arrow was training to be a medicine man. Delivering babies was part of his job."

Sal forced himself to remain calm even as fear surged through him. If he was scared, it must be a hundred times worse for Lulu. She needed him to be strong for her and the baby. Panicking wouldn't help anything. The confident expressions on Maura and Arrow's faces eased his trepidation a little.

"Well, ok," Sal said. "I trust you both, so if you say you can do it, then you can."

Lulu swallowed hard. "What if something goes wrong? Can you take care of whatever might happen?"

Maura said, "We'll all work together and make sure you're both fine. Don't be scared."

"I'll try," Lulu said. Another contraction gripped her, and she latched onto Sal's thigh.

Arrow and Maura hid their smiles at the pained expression on his face as Lulu exerted great force. Both Lulu and Sal groaned.

"Why are you groaning?" Lulu asked, her teeth clenched.

"Oh, no reason," Sal replied. "I'm just glad that's my thigh and not up higher or we wouldn't be having any more babies."

Arrow and Maura broke into laughter, and Lulu laughed through her pain. When the contraction eased, so did her grip, and both of them sagged in relief.

"We need to take a look," Arrow said.

Sal didn't like the idea of his brother-in-law being so familiar with his wife, but there was no way around that. "Ok," he said. "I guess I'm getting kicked out now. I'll be just outside."

Lulu grabbed his hand. "Where are you going? You're staying right here. Other husbands do it, and so are you."

His black eyebrows rose. "You want me to stay?"

"Yes. Marvin and Shadow Earnest did it. You're just as strong as they are, right?"

Sal still didn't like Marvin and Shadow very much, despite the fact that they'd assisted in keeping Arrow and Vanna safe last summer when the military wanted to take Arrow to a reservation. Lulu knew how to get to her husband. He couldn't resist a challenge and hated being bested at anything.

"Of course I am. You're right. I'll stay. What do I do?"

Maura and Arrow didn't know, since they hadn't had a man present at the birth of his baby before.

"I think you just hold her hand and keep her calm," Arrow said. "She must do most of the work, so we have to do whatever else we can to help her."

He and Maura checked Lulu's progress. Their professional approach put Lulu and Sal more at ease. Although he hid it well, Arrow was anxious and continually prayed for guidance in his mind. It had been a while since he'd delivered a baby, but he was determined that he and Maura would safely bring this baby into the world.

Maura said, "You'll be ready soon. Just rest when you can."

Lulu nodded. "Ok. I will."

Sal kissed her forehead. "I'll be right here. There's nothing we can't do together, Lulu, including this. So don't be scared. We've got a midwife and a medicine man and that's just as good as a doctor and a veterinarian. Hey, Arrow's a vet apprentice! So that's another thing in our favor. I'd say the odds are great and you know I never lose at anything."

Lulu laughed. "That's true; you don't. Especially when you cheat at hide-and-go-seek."

"Hey, that was just strategy. There's no rule sayin' that you gotta go far away from the base," he said.

They argued, teasing each other about it until the hard labor began. All of their concentration became focused on the task at hand. Sal got caught up helping Lulu, bathing her face with cold water and helping her lean forward to push. Lulu gained strength from his encouragement, and her natural instincts to bear down and work to bring forth their child took over. She ached to hold their baby, and that determination, along with Sal's help, kept her going.

Sylvia also assisted by bringing whatever Maura and Arrow needed. She was surprised yet proud that Sal had elected to stay with Lulu. The family stayed close by, either pacing out in the hall or sitting in an empty bedroom across the hall. Nick and Gino paced, Vanna simply sat, drumming her fingers on her lap, but Alfredo calmly read a book. He'd been through this four times, and although he was anxious, he knew that constantly fretting wouldn't help.

It might appear as though he wasn't paying attention, but he was aware of every noise that escaped the birthing room. It was the same as when Ming Li had been in labor with Jake. Nick hadn't been with her and Alfredo remembered him kneeling and praying for hours until Alfredo had made him get up and sit in a chair.

Nick, too, thought about Jake's birth, and he prayed that Sal and Lulu's baby would be healthy just like Jake had been. He also hoped that Lulu wouldn't have any complications. He smiled to himself as he remembered holding Jake for the first time. His throat constricted with tears as grief stabbed at him, but he refused to give into it, instead concentrating on the joy that was unfolding.

Lulu gripped her knees as Sal helped support her while she pushed.

"Don't stop," Maura urged. "Just a little more!"

Digging down even further, Lulu found more strength and strained harder, grunting as she put her heart and soul into the action. Even more intense pain struck her, immediately followed by a release in the tension as another little Terranova life was born.

Arrow said, "You can relax now." He grinned at them as he quickly cut the umbilical cord. "She's beautiful."

"She! We have a she! I mean a daughter!" Sal shouted, hugging an exhausted, but happy Lulu. He kissed her and laughed a little. "Oh, I love you so much."

"I love you, too," Lulu said as the baby let loose with a lusty cry. "She sounds just like you."

Maura and Arrow laughed while Sal scowled. He soon smiled again when Maura laid the baby in Lulu's arms.

"She's so perfect and beautiful," Lulu said, gazing at the baby's tiny face with love. "She has your black hair."

Sal touched the soft down on the baby's head. "Yeah, but she has your nose. I've never seen anything so beautiful," he said, getting choked up. "And I'm so glad I stayed. All men should. I know they're not really supposed to, I guess, but they should. The ones that don't, don't know what they're missin'."

Lulu smiled at him. "I'm so happy you did, too. Thank you."

"No thanks needed, honey."

Arrow said, "Ok, Pop. Go show her off."

Sal's brow furrowed. "Pop?" Then it dawned on him. "Oh! That's me now. *I'm* Pop!"

Lulu giggled at his startled excitement. "Yes, you are."

"And that makes you Mama," he said, taking the baby from Lulu. "Hello, little one. I'm your Pop and I love you."

Tears formed in Lulu's eyes as she watched Sal smile and speak tenderly to their daughter. The pride in his expression touched her heart and she fell in love all over again with her husband.

He kissed Lulu. "We'll be back. Maura, Arrow, we can't thank you enough. We're in your debt."

"No, you're not," Maura said. "We're family and glad to share this happy time with you."

Sal smiled at her and took the baby out of the room, where their family quietly exclaimed over her, congratulated the new father and asked how Lulu was doing. Sal assured them that Lulu had been strong and was well.

Sal looked at Nick. "C'mon, Nick. Hold your niece. Serena Sylvana Terranova, meet your Uncle Nick."

Nick was surprised that he was the first one Sal wanted to hold the baby. He'd thought it would be Alfredo or Sylvia. "Me?"

Smiling, Sal said, "Yeah, you. C'mon, Nicky."

Nick carefully took the baby from Sal, and an instant mixture of joy and nostalgia washed through him as he settled Serena in his arms. He played with one of her tiny fists, remembering how he'd done the same thing with Jake. "Hello, Serena. I'm glad to finally meet you. You kept teasin' us. Just like your old man. I hope that doesn't mean that you're gonna be as difficult as he is. Not to mention aggravating, stubborn, and egotistical."

"Hey!" Sal said loudly.

Serena's little forehead puckered, and she howled her objection to the sudden noise.

Nick kissed her forehead, and handed her back to Sal. "You made her cry, you make her stop," he said, smiling, while the rest of the family laughed.

Sal glowered at Nick as he bounced Serena a little and hummed softly to her and swayed back and forth. Serena soon quieted and Sal shot Nick a triumphant look.

Vanna laughed. "He's even competitive about calming a baby."

"Whose side are you on, Noodle?" Sal asked.

"You've had her long enough, Sal. My turn," Sylvia said.

Sal reluctantly relinquished Serena. "You do know that I'm the father."

"That's right," Sylvia said. "And you're gonna have her all the time. So we get her for right now." Tears trickled from her eyes. "She's so precious, Sally. Yes, you are, Serena. Nonna's been waiting for you, but now that you're here, you have to stay little for a long time, ok?"

All of them were anxious to hold the baby and she was passed along before she had to go back to her mama. As Sal took her back into their suite, Sylvia noted Nick's wistful expression as he watched them go.

"I'm gonna go make us all something to eat," he said. His happiness for Sal and Lulu was great, but he couldn't quite dispel the sadness that would always be in his soul. Cooking was his refuge when he was upset, and it would help him concentrate on something besides that grief.

"I'll be along to help you in a bit," Sylvia said. "I want to freshen up a little." She knew he needed a little space.

Nick nodded. "Ok."

As Nick walked down the hall away from them, they all exchanged sympathetic glances before going their separate ways.

Chapter Eight

When Gino showed up at the Hanovers' that evening, he almost didn't recognize Carrie when Gwen showed him into the parlor. She sat on the floor with Fi, playing paper dolls. Instead of a loose blouse and skirt, the white shirtwaist fit more snugly above her maroon wool skirt. It showed off the curvy figure he'd discerned the previous night when they'd gone dancing, and Gino felt a little warmer as he looked at her.

Carrie smiled as she rose from the floor to greet him. His appreciation made her glad that she'd decided to change the way she'd been dressing. "Hello," she said. "I wasn't sure when we'd see you again."

"Hi. I'm sorry about that. I was gonna drop by earlier today, but Lulu had the baby today, so I was caught up in that," he said, sitting in a chair once she'd sat on the sofa.

"That's wonderful!" Carrie said. "What did she have?"

"A girl. They named her Serena."

Fi scooted over to Gino using her strong arms and one good leg. She reached up to him and he picked her up, sitting her on his lap. "I'll bet she's pretty. Can I see her?"

"Of course," Gino said. "Tomorrow you and Mommy can come out for dinner and visit. Would you like that?"

Fi nodded. "Yeah. Guess what?"

"What?"

"I'm going to school tomorrow. I met Adam and the other kids today and they were really nice," she said. "I even made another friend already."

Gino smiled. "That's great. I'm not surprised a nice girl like you would make friends quick."

Carrie said, "She made friends with Mia Wu the other day when we went for Fi's appointment, and now Lucky's son asked if she could go to their farm this weekend."

Fi nodded. "He's gonna teach me Cheyenne, and him and Mia are gonna help me ride Basco again to make my leg stronger."

"Wow. Sounds like a good time," Gino said.

Carrie said, "You should come with us."

"I'd like that," he said. It would be fun. "What time?"

"Lucky said to come anytime. He's going to cook that night," Carrie said.

"He's a good cook," Gino said. "He makes a lot of Indian and Irish food. How about I pick you up around three on Saturday?"

"That'll be fine, lad," Fi said in an Irish brogue. "Da used to say stuff like that."

Gino smiled. "I'll bet he was a fun dad."

"Aye, he was," she said, making them laugh.

Carrie said, "Lucky reminds me of him so much."

"I'll bet," Gino said.

"I miss Da, but he's in heaven with all of the angels. I'll see him someday again," Fi said. "Who does the baby look like?" she asked abruptly.

"Like both Sal and Lulu. Her hair is black, but she definitely has Lulu's nose. We're not sure about her eye color, though. It's too soon."

Carrie was grateful that Fi had changed the subject. She, too, missed Aidan, but it wasn't nearly as sharp as it used to be. But hearing Fi talk about him brought that grief closer to the surface. She didn't want to cry in front of either Fi or Gino.

"Gino, do you know anyone who's hiring right now?" she asked.

It should have occurred to him that she would need work. He didn't know the state of her finances, but he was betting that she wasn't rich by any means. Gino didn't consider himself sexist, but for some reason the idea of Carrie working bothered him. It shouldn't. The women in his family all worked outside the home. Without someone else to support her and Fi, it fell to Carrie to do it, of course.

"Not right now, but you should look in the paper," he said. He didn't want to worry her in front of Carrie, so he didn't mention that jobs were still hard to come by in Echo.

She smiled and said, "Right." She'd done that, but there had only been one listed, and when she'd gone to enquire about it, it had already been taken.

"Mommy, may I have some peaches?" she asked.

Carrie had bought some tins of fruit at the store, because she knew how much Fi liked it. "You certainly may. Come to the kitchen with me," she said.

She handed Fi her crutches, and Gino steadied her on them before letting her go. He smiled at her chatter, and she and Carrie went out to the kitchen. Resting back against his chair, he contemplated some things. He needed to talk to Carrie alone, and decided that since Fi would go to school in the morning, he could stop by after school started.

Carrie came back into the parlor just as Gino yawned. "Well, someone's tired."

"Yeah. Mama got me up around three to let me know that Lulu was in labor. I'm not complainin', though. Being there was great. Watchin' Sal with Serena was really touching. The same when we went to visit with Lulu a little." Gino grinned. "Arrow and Maura delivered her."

"They did? Why?" Carrie asked, surprised.

"Erin and Win were doing surgery and our pastor, Andi Thatcher, isn't back in town yet. She was a nurse in the Salvation Army and she helps out with medical stuff sometimes. Arrow was training to be a medicine man with his tribe and has delivered babies before. Maura was a midwife when she lived with the Comanche. So between the two of them, the birth went just fine. Erin checked them both over today, pronounced them healthy and said they did a great job," Gino explained.

"I'm so glad it all turned out so well," she said.

"Me, too. Are you busy around nine tomorrow morning?"

"No."

"Ok. I thought I'd show you around some more," Gino said.

Carrie was happy that he wanted to spend so much time with her and Fi. "I'd like that."

Gino yawned and stood. "I guess I'd better go get some sleep."

She understood, but was sorry to see him go so soon. "I'd say that's a good idea."

He smiled. "I'll go say goodnight to Fi." He walked out to the kitchen. "How are those peaches?"

Fi had a mouthful, so she nodded.

"Good. That new baby had us all up early, so I'm bushed. I'm gonna go home, but I'll see you tomorrow afternoon, ok?" he asked.

"All right," she said. "I can't wait to see the baby."

"She's a cutie," Gino said. Bending, he kissed her forehead. "Have a good night, Fi."

To his surprise, Fi wound her arms around Gino's neck. "Ok, Mr. Terranova. You, too."

Hugging her back, Gino felt tears prick the backs of his eyes. "How about you just call me Gino?"

"Ok, Gino." She released him and kissed his cheek again.

The tender exchange between them brought a lump to Carrie's throat. She swallowed and said, "I'll be right back, Fi."

"All right."

She walked to the front door with Gino. "She really likes you."

Gino said, "I'm glad." He looked around to make sure that no one else was around. "I think maybe her mommy might like me a little, too."

Carrie arched an eyebrow. "And what makes you think that?"

Gino whispered, "Your kiss last night."

His rakish smile and shining eyes made her giggle a little. “I don’t remember any kiss,” she whispered back.

“Hmm. I’ll remind you again sometime, but for now ...” He kissed her cheek quickly. “Goodnight, *deserto fiore*.”

Carrie couldn’t stop smiling as she closed the door after him. She had to take a moment to get her giddiness under control before going to check on Fi.

Andi watched her father look around the church, nervous about what he might think of it. She knew it was silly, but his opinion was important to her. A church was about the people more so than the building, but she still wanted him to like it. Bea and her daughter kept it spotless, and the pine pews gleamed from their regular polishing. There were some colorful cushions scattered around for people who preferred them, and thanks to a generous donation from the Terranovas, they had new bibles.

Levi noticed the frown of worry between Andi’s eyes, and he remembered feeling that way about his first church when he’d been a young pastor. He was extraordinarily proud of his daughter, and he’d never tried to stand in her way. After her near-death experience, he’d seen a new light in her, and when she’d announced at the age of fifteen that she was going to be a pastor, he’d known without a doubt that she’d been called.

He ran a hand over the beautiful piano. “You must be getting some nice collections to be able to afford a piece like that.”

“Actually, Marvin and Shadow Earnest donated it. They performed one Sunday and saw the condition of the old one and the next thing I know, a brand new one is delivered,” she said.

“Oh, yes. The Earnests. The ones you told me have such dark souls.”

“Had. Their souls are much lighter these days, but the darkness won’t ever be completely gone. I haven’t invaded their privacy, but I know something horrible happened to them for such darkness to be inside of them. They’re good men, but they don’t know it or always believe it. I’m not sure which,” she said.

Levi put an arm around her shoulders. "I'm sure you had a lot to do with that lightening of their souls. You have such a way with people."

"I had a great teacher."

He smiled at her. "Well, I'm going to go over to the parsonage and work on my sermon for Sunday."

"Thank you so much for filling in for me until Arliss and I get back," Andi said. "There's no one else who would take as good care of my flock as you will."

"I'm honored that you asked me." He gave her another squeeze. "All right. I'm off, but I'll see you later on."

"Ok, Dad. Let me know if you need anything," Andi said.

"I will."

As he left, Levi's approval of her church left Andi with a warm feeling. Then, she went to finish some work that she wanted to clear away before the wedding. *I'm finally marrying my men!* Andi giggled aloud as she thought about their impending nuptials. She went to her office, her heart filled with joy.

Dropping Fi off at school was hard for Carrie because she was worried about how she'd get around, but Adam assured her that he'd take good care of her. Otto was also a little gentleman and told her that he'd help her. She could see that his parents were raising a fine boy. She'd forced herself to leave the school. Fi had to learn independence and going to school was the first step in that direction.

She stopped by the *Echo Express* and bought a newspaper to read while she waited for Gino to arrive. Looking at the help wanted ads, there were only a couple of postings for ranch hands and the like. Nothing that she was skilled at. She needed work, and she wanted to find a place to live. The boarding house was nice, but she wanted a home.

Molly Watson, co-owner, editor and chief reporter of the newspaper wrote interesting articles, but Carrie couldn't concentrate on them, because she was nervous about what Gino wanted to discuss. Maybe he'd decided that things weren't going to work out between them. Although after his playfulness the night before, she didn't really think that was the case. She could speculate all day, but it wasn't doing her any good. Trying to calm her nerves, she put more effort in reading the articles, but her uncertainty didn't completely abate. Nine o'clock couldn't come soon enough.

Earlier that morning, Gino asked Sylvia to speak with him privately. They went to the Lion's Den to talk. This was what they called their large conference room/office.

"What's on your mind, Gino?" she asked.

"I need your advice as a woman."

"All right. Go ahead."

Gino fidgeted a little. "Carrie needs to find work. She asked me if I knew anyone who was hiring, but I don't. You know what the job situation is like around here. As soon as a job is available, it's taken. I'm worried that she's gonna run out of money before she finds a job. I'd give her money, but I doubt she'd take it."

Sylvia tapped the table with her fingers. "I'm sure her funds are limited. It doesn't sound as though her husband was rich, and even if she is an accountant, it might be hard to find work since a lot of places still don't consider women capable of such a job. I know that look, Gino. You always look that way when you've got an idea."

"As a woman, put yourself in Carrie's position. We've only known each other a few days. If you were her and I proposed to you, would you accept?" he asked.

Sylvia smiled. "Let me ask you a few questions before I answer that."

"Ok."

"Are you attracted to her?"

Gino nodded. "Yeah. She's fun, pretty, and smart. She's a great mother and a good person."

"So you don't pity her?"

"No," Gino replied. "Not at all. I admire her for the way she's taken care of Fi and kept them afloat after losing Aidan. I know she loved him very much. I don't mean this in a bad way, but I find myself wanting to take care of them. Is that a bad thing?"

Sylvia said, "Not at all. That's the sign of a man who'll make a good husband. Most men are protective of their women and want to take care of them. Your father has always been like that. It's one of the reasons he's worked so hard to get us where we are today. He wanted to take good care of his family and he has. I know you wanting to do that for Carrie and Fi isn't meant in a disrespectful way."

"No, it's not. Fi's a special little girl and Carrie's a special woman for taking care of her the way she does. She's strong, too, to have done it mostly on her own," Gino said.

Sylvia chuckled. "Yes, little Fiona touched our hearts right away, too. She's so pleasant, even with her weak leg. She's sweet and funny. I don't think it would be too hard having her as a granddaughter," she said, winking at Gino. "And you can work on making me more grandbabies to hold and love."

Gino shook his head and laughed. "I swear you just want us all to get married so we have grandbabies for you."

She laughed. "No, I want you all to be happy. Gino, what is your heart telling you to do?"

"I've been asking myself that question ever since yesterday. I don't think I love her. It's too soon for that, but I strongly like her. I've never wanted to ask a woman to marry me, but I want to ask Carrie to. It's crazy, but I do," Gino said.

"Then you should ask her. She *did* come here to marry you. Chelsea was a fool for not trying a relationship with you. I didn't say so to her, but she passed up a good, handsome, smart man. I think Carrie's a lot smarter than that," Sylvia told him.

Gino said, "I was really irritated at the time, but now I'm thinkin' that she wasn't who I'm meant to be with. So you really think I should propose?"

"Yes, I do."

Gino was quiet a moment, just looking at Sylvia. Then said, "I'm gonna do it, Mama. I'm gonna ask her to marry me."

Sylvia clasped her hands together. "I'm so happy for you."

"Wait to be happy until she accepts," Gino said. "Don't jinx me."

"You're right. I'll pray that she says yes," Sylvia said.

Now that he'd decided, Gino was excited and nervous. "I don't know how to ask her. I want it to be special. Any suggestions?"

Sylvia took his hand. "Gino, what matters most to a woman is that a proposal is from the heart and I know that you don't love her, but she'll see that you respect and like her and for a woman in her position, that's gonna mean a lot. We don't need a lot of fancy stuff. It's nice, but it's not necessary."

"Thanks, Mama. I knew you'd have good advice. You always do." He kissed her cheek and stood up. "I gotta go to town. I'll see you later on."

Sylvia waited a couple of minutes before going to find Alfredo to tell him. Her soul was filled with happiness that her only unmarried child may have found his mate. "Oh, Heavenly Father, please let it be so," she said in Italian, as she put on her coat and hurried out to the barn.

Chapter Nine

At nine o'clock, a knock came on the front door, but the caller wasn't Gino. Instead, Vanna called out to Carrie.

Carrie went to the foyer. "Vanna? How nice to see you."

Vanna said, "It's nice to see you, too. Gino got held up doing something, but he wanted me to give you this." She held out a plain, sealed envelope.

Perplexed and curious, Carrie took it. "Thank you, Vanna. How do you like being Aunt Vanna?"

Vanna's dark eyes lit up. "I love it. Serena's such a sweet baby. It's so nice to have a baby in the house again. I can't wait until Arrow and I have a baby."

"I'm sure it won't be long," Carrie said.

Vanna winked at her. "I'm sure, too. I'll see you and Fi tonight."

"See you then." Carrie chuckled as Vanna left.

As she opened the envelope, she wondered what was making Gino run behind.

Carrie,

Sorry for being late, but I had something come up unexpectedly. I thought about it and I know someone who is looking for someone with your skills. There's a test included in the envelope from him. He also wants to meet with you at Mama T's at eleven o'clock for an interview, but only if you answer all of the problems. I'll see you sometime after that. Good luck on the test.

Gino

Two other papers were in the envelope on which various complicated math problems were written. Anticipation filled her as she took the envelope up to her room and started the test right away. Each numerical answer would correspond with a letter in the alphabet, thereby revealing a message to her.

The problems were intricate and she had a good time working her way through them. She'd always loved math and the exercise was fun for her whereas some people wouldn't have understood the first thing about the algebraic problems. She wrote the correct alphabet letter as she went. After the eighth problem, she looked at what was on her paper.

"W I L L Y O U M" was written in her neat hand. "Willyoum? What does that spell? That would be a strange way to spell William." She solved two more problems, adding an A and an R. "Willyoumar," she repeated a couple of times. Then her mind began breaking the letters up in to word groupings. "Will you mar—no, that would be silly for a potential employer to ask me to marry him." By the time she'd completed the remaining problems the question, "Will you marry me?" was indeed the message.

She shook her head. "I don't understand. Why on Earth would a complete stranger ask me to marry him? Has he even seen me before? Maybe he's just being humorous. I hope so."

Ruminating on the situation, she changed into a more business-like gray skirt suit and a stylish black hat. Whoever this man was, she was only showing up because Gino had recommended the position to her and she needed a job.

"Well, Mystery Man, don't get your hopes up for any nuptials," she said, smiling as she left for the restaurant.

Entering Mama T.'s, she saw that it was empty of diners. Walking a little further inside, she saw a man sitting with his back to her at a table in the rear of the dining room near the kitchen.

"Hello?" she called.

The man rose and turned to face her. With a shock she realized that the man in the elegant deep blue suit was Gino. Dumbstruck she could only watch as he strode towards her with amusement in his eyes. He looked so handsome and suave as he moved.

"Hello, Carrie. I see you passed the test," he said.

"I don't understand," she said. "I thought there was a job interview."

"In a sense there is," Gino said. "Did you understand the question?"

"Yes, I did, but I thought it was just a strange way to break the ice," she said.

Gino smiled. "No, the question is real."

She felt a little faint as she realized that the proposal was serious. "I, um, well, oh boy."

Her suddenly pale pallor alarmed Gino. "Are you ok? Here, sit down."

Carrie sat down in the chair he guided her to at the table where he'd been sitting. He gave her a glass of water and she took a sip. "I'm all right. Just stunned. This is so completely unexpected."

Gino pulled his chair over close to hers. "I know it is, but I think we're compatible. We share a lot of the same interests, I respect you as a person and you're a wonderful mother. You've come through a terrible couple of years, but you stayed strong. You're brave for taking the chance to come here to meet me. You're beautiful and judging by that kiss, we're attracted to each other."

"That's all true, but what about Fiona?"

"What about her?" Gino asked.

"Are you completely serious about taking her on? I don't want you to regret marrying me or becoming her stepfather," Carrie said, her eyes locked on his.

Gino smiled. "You don't just 'take on' kids like Fi. You take them into your heart. She's a special little girl and I'd never regret being her stepfather. And, I doubt that I would ever regret marrying you, either." He took her hands and knelt on one knee. "I promise to always take care of you and Fi. I'll always respect you and I'll be the best possible husband and father I can. I take commitment seriously and you'll never have to doubt my fidelity. Carrie, *ti sposerà me*? Will you marry me?"

Conviction and promise was reflected in Gino's eyes, showing Carrie how serious he was, despite his playful way of proposing to her. She could envision a life with him and his big, warm and funny family. And they would be so good for Fiona, too.

Squeezing his hands back, she smiled and said, "Yes, Gino, I'll marry you."

Happiness flowed through him and Gino kissed her hand before releasing them so he could retrieve a ring box from his suit jacket. Opening it, he said, "This was Mama's ring. She would've given it to Nick, but he wanted to get his first wife, Ming Li, something to reflect her Japanese culture, so she gave it to me as the second oldest son."

The white opal ring with diamond accents was exquisite and Carrie's breath caught in her throat as he slipped it on her. "It's beautiful. I'm so honored to wear it, Gino."

He kissed her hand again and sat back in his chair. "I'm so glad it fits. We'll get it resized if necessary."

"No, it's perfect."

Their eyes met and held. Gino leaned closer and pressed a soft kiss to her lips. Keeping in mind that they were in a public place with several people back in the kitchen, he resisted the temptation to continue kissing her, instead pulling back and smiling at Carrie.

"I'm so happy," she said.

"Me, too. I guess I'll let the folks back there know that the coast is clear. I hope you're hungry. I thought a nice brunch might be a nice way to celebrate."

"I'd love that," she said.

"Good. I'll be right back," Gino said.

When he tried to push the right side of the double doors of the kitchen in, it banged against something and he heard Nick say, "Ow!"

Entering, Gino said, "Serves you right for eavesdropping."

Nick rubbed his ear and frowned at him. "I was just making sure no customers were comin' in."

"Tsk, tsk, Nicky. You shouldn't lie," Gino said, smiling.

Sylvia said, "Enough, boys! What did she say?"

Gino said, "Well, she said she'd think about it."

"Think about it?" Nick asked. "She came here to marry you. What's there to think about?"

"That's right," Sylvia said.

Their indignant attitudes made it impossible for Gino to keep a straight face. He laughed and said, "I was just kiddin'. She said yes."

"Shame on you!" Sylvia said, swatting his arm.

Then, she and Nick hugged him. Tyler and Allie, the wait staff and their new daytime kitchen helper, Jonas Hart, congratulated him. They all followed Gino out to the dining room to congratulate Carrie and welcome her to the family.

"I'm so honored to wear your lovely ring," Carrie said to Sylvia. "I'll treasure it."

"It looks good on you," Sylvia said, kissing her cheek. "Now, you two sit down. Your brunch will be ready in just a few minutes. C'mon, everyone. Let's get their meal."

She shooed the others into the kitchen to see to it and Carrie chuckled. "Your family is so much fun."

Gino said, "We have our moments. Mama rules the kitchen at home, but Nick's in charge here for the most part. She doesn't mind tellin' all of us what to do at home, but she can't do it with other people. Nick doesn't have that trouble, though. He keeps on top of things. They do almost all of the cooking at home except for lunch."

"Oh," Carrie said. "What if someone else wants to cook?"

Gino hadn't thought of that, but knew he should have. "Feel free to cook whenever you want to. Just let them know when you want to so they don't already plan something. You'll have to make plenty because we're all big eaters. I'm sure one of the other girls would like helping you since cooking with Mama and Nick is impossible. I've tried, so I know. Pop and I cook when they're not around, but they're too fussy and always telling us what we're doing wrong. It's nerve wracking."

Carrie smiled at the image of Gino fighting with his mother and brother over making meals. "Maybe you and I could cook together."

Gino grinned. "I'd like that. I think that would be fun."

In a few minutes, their brunch arrived and they spent the meal talking about what sorts of things they would make together, and how they could have Fi help them. As they did, they were drawn closer, and both of them were optimistic about what the days ahead held for them.

Chapter Ten

Andi could hardly contain her excitement as she checked her appearance in the mirror in her bedroom. Lulu had designed and made the high-necked, white lace pearl adorned dress for her. The seamstress had designed the dress with a moderately full skirt, which looked better on Andi's tall frame. Vanna had swept her rich, brown hair back from her face in an intricate chignon that wouldn't interfere with Andi's veil.

"You look spectacular," Bea said. "Your men will be bowled over."

Marvin had relieved her of her playing duties so that she could enjoy being Andi's maid of honor.

"Are you sure?" Andi asked.

Vanna, Lulu and Erin, her bridesmaids, all answered in the affirmative.

"All right." Andi's stomach tightened with nerves.

Bea said, "We should go over to the church so we don't run into Arliss."

"Ok. I don't want any bad luck." Andi took a deep breath. "I'm ready."

Erin said, "Let's go get you married."

Excitement flooded her being. "Yes, let's."

Nora fussed over Arliss' appearance, straightening his tie and making sure his tuxedo was lint-free. "You boys look so handsome. R.J., Win did such a nice job with your hair."

"He always does, Mother," R.J. replied. "I wasn't about to let us look shaggy on such an important day. But Arliss didn't fight me—for once."

Lucky, their best man, said, "I told him he'd better look presentable, or I was gonna hold him down for Win so he could cut it."

Arliss said, "I'd like to see you try it."

"We'll see about that sometime," Lucky responded.

Wild Wind, his groomsman chuckled. "I can't wait to see that."

Levi entered the church basement. "Hello everyone. May I have a word with the grooms, please? Go on up to the altar, and we'll be along soon."

"Right," Lucky said.

Arliss' parents and the rest left the basement.

When they'd gone, Levi said, "I've never met anyone like you and I was confused when I first arrived. I had serious reservations about you and Andi marrying. Andi said to give it time before making any judgments, and to keep an open mind. I'm glad I did.

"I've watched you with her and I can see how important she is to you. You're a gentleman, and the fact that you've been together all of this time and haven't tried to seduce her tells me that you respect her. I've come to know each of you, and I see that you're each your own person and yet the same person. Andi said I would come to understand, and I have.

"I like each of you for different reasons. I think God picked you for Andi because He knew that you would accept her and understand about her unusual abilities. It's not every man who would choose to marry a female pastor who has some strong psychic abilities. In short, you're a unique bunch of good men, and I thank you for loving my little girl and making her so happy."

Arliss said, "Sir, it's an honor to be marrying Andi. She believed in us and helped us right from the start. She somehow understood us right away and never belittled me for my condition. I hate calling it that, because I love my brothers. Anyway, we love her more every day and we'll always do anything to make her happy and to protect her. We'll be good providers, too. We're hoping that it won't be long before kids come along, too. We promise to take good care of her. Thank you for entrusting us with her and it's an honor to have you performing the ceremony, too."

The two men shook hands before Levi said, "It's an honor to be officiating, too, and in my daughter's own church. I'm so proud of her. Well, we should go on up."

Arliss grinned. "We're ready."

Levi smiled and led the way up the stairs.

Arliss, Lucky, and Wild Wind stood up at the altar. They were surprised when a bunch of people began filing into the choir box. Billy, Keith, Henley's sister, Lyla, and several others had been coaxed into joining the choir, and the seats were quickly filled. They were further surprised to see Henley stand in front of the choir box, ready to direct the singers.

Once Marvin was in place, he played a note on his pitch pipe for each of the five parts. It looked comical when he raised his violin bow and nodded to Marvin to begin. Marvin played the intro and Henley brought the choir in right on cue. The congregation listened in amazement to the beautiful performance. It had been a long time since a full choir had performed in the church and the experience brought tears to the eyes of some of the older members as they listened.

In her office, Andi heard it and at first she thought she was having a vision. The other women heard it, too.

"What's going on out there?" she asked.

Bea smiled. "It's your wedding present from your choir. Come listen."

She cracked the door open, making sure that Arliss wasn't around anywhere, and then motioned Andi and Erin into the narthex with her. Shadow and Bree had offered for their twins, Rory and Lucas, to serve as the flower girl and ring bearer. Bree and the twins had also been in the office with them and followed them into the narthex. The doors to the sanctuary were closed so that Andi couldn't see her groom, but the music came through loud and clear.

As she listened, Andi knew that there were more people than the seven original members singing. It was a full, rich sound that made Andi's heart swell with love for all those singing, and for whomever had put it all together. She closed her eyes and swayed to the music, letting it fill her with joy and light. As she did, all of her anxiety melted away to be replaced by excited anticipation.

She jerked a little when she felt someone take her hand. Then, she realized it was her father and opened her eyes.

He smiled at her. "I know I'm technically supposed to wait for the reception, but will you dance with me?"

She grinned at him. "Yes, of course. I think we can defy convention a little."

As they danced, Levi said, "That's some choir you have there and the boy directing it is outstanding. Where did you find him?"

"Boy? What boy?" she asked.

"A redheaded fellow. Tall and gangly?"

Her eyes widened. "That's Henley Remington. Why is he directing the choir? He's a musical prodigy, so I'm not surprised he'd do a good job."

Levi chuckled. "Well, whatever happened, I'd say it's a godsend. I wish your mother could see you. You know how proud she was of you, honey."

Andi blinked away tears. "I wish she was here, too, but she's watching, Dad. I feel her."

He nodded as the song ended, and they stopped dancing.

"Are all of you ready?" he asked.

The door opened, and the twins began walking down the aisle. They had Bree's brown hair and Shadow's blue eyes. Rory threw the flower petals around instead of on the floor, and some of congregation members got a flower shower. Bree quickly came behind her, stopping Rory, while Lucas continued on to the altar.

He walked over to Lucky and handed him the little pillow with the rings on it. "These are for you. Don't drop that. Bye," he said.

Marvin looked at Shadow, and they grinned at each other over his bossiness. Bree guided Rory the rest of the way down the aisle, collected Lucas and took them to where they were sitting.

Erin began walking down the aisle while Marvin played a pretty piece of classical music instead of the Wedding March. Bea followed her and they took their place at the altar. As Levi and Andi came down the aisle, her gaze was trained on Arliss. His eye met hers and she swore that she could see her men rapidly coming to the fore and fading back.

Darlin', you're the most beautiful woman on Earth.

You're stunning, love.

Mmm mmm mmm.

Their words came to her clearly and she smiled at him, thinking him the most handsome man she'd ever seen. His sandy, brown hair was styled neatly and his tuxedo made his fine physique look even more impressive. Arliss gave her a knowing smile, indicating that he understood that she'd received their messages.

Levi saw their silent communication and smiled. *Yes, my daughter has picked well.* Arriving at the altar, Levi stopped Andi and lifted her veil. Normally, the groom would have lifted it before he kissed his bride, but Arliss hadn't wanted anything to obstruct his view of Andi's eyes as they said their vows. Levi arranged the veil and kissed both of Andi's cheeks. Giving Arliss her hand, he whispered, "You'll all have to take turns holding her hands."

Arliss and Andi smiled as Levi went up a couple of steps and began the ceremony. Arliss' mind spun with all of the emotions inside him at that moment. When he tried very hard, he was able to erect a wall between his and Andi's mind. He put it up because he didn't want to distract her. They'd never felt so much joy, love and peace as when they were with Andi.

This beautiful woman who'd shown them such kindness and who accepted them in every way was about to become theirs forever. Her brown-sugar eyes shone with love as they said their vows. Andi loved that all three brothers took rotating turns as they were said. It was fitting that they each have a part in the ceremony.

When they came to the ring exchange, Arliss teared up a little when he put Andi's on her finger. Seeing his ring on her finger gave him more satisfaction and happiness than he could have imagined, and his brothers felt the same. When she slid Arliss' on, Andi looked into his eyes and had to blink away her own tears. God had sent her three-in-one men to her and had taken them from her for a short time before giving them back to her. She appreciated and loved them all the more, determined to make every moment with them count.

Levi's voice was a little thick as he said, "I now pronounce you man and wife. You may now kiss your bride."

Arliss had intended to keep their kiss chaste, but one brush of her soft lips against his did him in. He pulled her into his embrace and kissed her soundly. Levi tapped on his shoulder repeatedly and cleared his throat.

Lucky said, "Excuse me for sayin' so, Reverend, but she *is* kissin' all three of them."

The congregation laughed, and the couple parted, Andi giving Arliss a slightly dazed smile. He'd let the wall down, pouring all of his love into the kiss and receiving the same from Andi. She wasn't the only who felt a little dizzy.

Arliss saw Levi looking at them with a disapproving frown, and they turned to face the congregation.

"I now present to you Mr. and Mrs. Arliss and company Jackson," Levi said, thinking it was the strangest presentation of a newlywed couple he'd ever performed.

The wedding guests applauded them, and the couple beamed as they walked up the aisle to the narthex where a reception line was created. All of the well-wishing was much appreciated, and Arliss loved watching Andi interact with everyone. She made people feel at ease, and he knew that she genuinely cared about each one of them.

Levi noted that Arliss was the one who mainly dealt with the congregation since he was the most spiritual out of the three brothers. However, whenever someone spoke directly to R.J. or Blake, they were answered by the appropriate personality. Arliss' rapid transformations amazed Levi.

The reception was held in the town hall auditorium, since there was plenty of room, and it wouldn't be appropriate for it to be held at a saloon. There wouldn't be any alcohol served except for the champagne for the toast, but there was plenty of delectable food to eat and Bea had enlisted Sylvia's help with making the cake, since as the maid of honor, she was busy helping make many of the arrangements. Bea had designed the gorgeous creation, but Sylvia had brought it to life.

They had barely arrived at the reception before Molly stopped them.

"Congratulations to all of you," she said. "Pastor Andi, how does it feel to be married to three men?" She was getting information for the wedding announcement.

Andi laughed as Arliss put an arm around her. Looking at him, she said, "It feels incredible. Every woman should marry three men."

Everyone around them laughed, and she realized how that sounded and blushed.

"Don't you dare print that," she told Molly.

The reporter smiled, and she asked the couple a few more questions before Keith pulled her away, telling her to let them alone. They visited and joked with everyone until the meal was ready.

Lucky got the guests' attention and said, "Thank youse for comin' to celebrate the weddin' of our good pastor and the three questionable lads she picked. Lord knows they try to be good, but it ain't easy for them. Of course, Arliss was always in trouble or causin' trouble or just attractin' it." Lucky saw Arliss' family laugh and nod their heads. "See? They agree with me, so I'm not lyin'.

"But even when he was bein' bad, Arliss was good. Good at pickin' pockets and good at poker, too. Good at drinkin' my beer when I wasn't lookin' and good at makin' my money disappear by connin' me into buyin' him drinks."

The guests laughed while Arliss put his head down on the table and banged his forehead lightly on it.

"Now, don't do that, lad. A reception is no fun with a passed out groom unless he's drunk so you can put him in funny positions."

More laughter followed his statement.

"Anyhow, while he used to be good at bein' bad, ever since he met Andi, it seems like he's gettin' better at being good. That's because he got smart, and hung onto a good woman with a generous heart and who liked the idea of bein' courted by three lads."

Andi blushed and laughed.

"Now, just think about that. What woman wouldn't want to be courted by three lads at once who love her to distraction? It means three times more kissin', three times more presents, and three times more dinners out. A woman would have to be crazy not to want that."

"Lucky!" Andi protested while laughing.

He grinned at her. "All right. But seriously, Andi has a way with Arliss, R.J., and Blake. Now with that one, it's like tamin' a lion, but it seems like Andi's whip does the job. Better keep a chair handy, too, Pastor." Blake glared at Lucky, who just grinned back. "I've had the pleasure of watchin' their romance, along with many of us, and Andi has truly gentled her men somewhat. And he's brought her happiness and fun. It's easy to see how much they love each other, and I wish them every happiness under the sun. Please raise your glasses and join me in toasting our newlyweds.

"May your mornings bring joy and your evenings bring peace. May your troubles grow few as your blessings increase. May the saddest day of your future be no worse than the happiest day of your past. May your hands be forever clasped in friendship and your hearts joined forever in love. Your lives are very special, God has touched you in many ways. May His blessings rest upon you and fill all your coming days."

Everyone drank to the toast and then Levi said the blessing so the meal could begin. As they ate, the newlyweds held hands a lot, and Arliss was hard-pressed not to at least kiss Andi's cheek. Once everyone had eaten their fill, the musicians and singers assembled and the dancing began.

R.J. was the best formal dancer, and took Andi in his arms to start the bride and groom dance. They elegantly waltzed around the dance area while they barely looked away from each other. Arliss and Blake also took turns, but R.J. finished up the dance, gracefully bowing and kissing her hand while the guests applauded.

Bea beamed as she watched them. She was so happy for her friends. They'd endured so much and it was wonderful to see their dream of marrying come true. She swayed a little with the music, humming along. After the father-daughter dance, the rest of the guests took the floor. Bea was surprised when Levi asked her to dance.

The pretty brunette didn't know what to say at first. It had been a long time since she'd had a man outside of a few of her friends ask her to dance.

Levi smiled at her, his warm, dark eyes gleaming. "Humor an old man, Mrs. Watson," he said coaxingly.

She returned his smile and said, "I'll humor you, but you're not much older than me, I'll wager."

He took her hand, led her out onto the floor, and they enjoyed themselves, talking and laughing together.

Andi noticed. "Look, honey. I've only seen Bea dance with someone a few times and I don't know when the last time was that Dad did."

Arliss said, "Now, darlin', don't go playin' matchmaker."

Her eyes shone brighter. "Wouldn't that be wonderful, though?"

He grinned. "I'm too late. The seed has already been planted."

"That's right. It has."

Soon, they cut the cake, and Andi's men ate two pieces of it, once they made sure that everyone had gotten some. They thanked Sylvia for making such a delicious confection. They also thanked everyone who'd sang in the choir. Andi cornered Henley.

"Marvin tells me that you told him that I asked you to take over the choir," she said. "I don't remember doing that."

Henley nodded. "Sure you did. You said that the choir needed help with settling disputes and making them into a cohesive unit."

Sometimes the way someone actually said something and what Henley heard were two different things.

Andi chuckled. "No, I said that they argued a lot, and that I wished they got along better."

"Right," Henley agreed. "A choir director helps the choir do that. So that's what I did."

She could see that she wasn't going to get anywhere with him. Once his mind was set, that was it. She chuckled. "Well, at any rate, I have to admit that you did a splendid job and as long as they don't object, it's all right with me if you continue on."

Henley smiled. "Great! We have a lot of fun."

Andi hugged him, and then she and Arliss moved on, saying their goodbyes and leaving.

Andi was surprised when Arliss took her hand and began leading her across the street instead of getting into their buggy.

"Where are we going? I thought we were leaving for Dickensville to get on the train tomorrow," she said.

"Well, I have a little surprise for you. We're spending the night in a very special place and then headin' out in the morning."

"We are?"

"Yep," he said, looking at her. "I think you'll like it."

She grew even more perplexed when they walked around back of the parsonage to the carriage house where he lived.

"I don't understand," she said, as he stopped her at the door.

He gave her a wink. "You will. Just stay here for a minute. I'll be right back."

Andi knew how much they all like planning surprises for her. She grew antsy with anticipation as she waited for him. When he returned, he left the door open and put his arms around her.

"Time to do my first duty as a groom and carry you over the threshold," he said.

"No, no! You can't carry me," she said. "I'm too ... big. You'll—" She let out a startled cry as he swooped her up in his arms and stepped into the carriage house.

Her jaw dropped open as she looked around at all of pretty candles that he'd lit around the little parlor. "It's beautiful."

"I'm glad you like it," he said. "We're gonna be living here and we wanted the first time we made love to be in our home."

The sweetness of his statement touched her heart and then she blushed, suddenly nervous. "You did?"

"Yeah. This is where we're gonna start our new life together, so it just seemed right that we start makin' kids here right away," he said.

Andi laughed and laid her head on his shoulder. He didn't move to put her down and she didn't request to be. He always made her feel feminine and pretty. Her height and strength didn't bother him at all; rather, he appreciated her shape. Finally she did have him put her down, but he did it slowly so that their bodies didn't lose contact.

The heat in his eyes set her heartbeat trotting along at a faster clip. His intense expression was reminiscent of Blake, but she understood that this was Arliss letting her finally see his powerful hunger for her; something he'd kept in check for so long out of deference to her. There was no escaping his smoldering gaze, and she didn't want to.

She couldn't move as he ran his hands up her arms, over her shoulders and neck, before cupping her face.

"We love you so much, Andi. We never thought we'd find someone like you. Lucky was right when he said that you've made us better men. You make us want to be better men, and we'll always support and love you in every way."

His kiss was slow, thorough and so sensual that it left her feeling a little dizzy. He completely let down the wall in his mind that he always tried to keep up when he kissed her, and it was a deeply moving experience to feel all of the passion he'd been holding back. Fire flowed through her as he kissed her again, pressing her closer against him.

Arliss hadn't been the only one keeping a tight rein on passion. It hadn't been easy for Andi to restrain the desire he stirred in her. As his hands moved down her back, his touch broke the dam of control inside her and she responded to him in a way she'd never allowed herself to before.

She unbuttoned his coat, and shoved it over his shoulders. He let his hands drop, so that he could take it off while she got rid of hers. He'd barely laid his coat on the sofa until Andi was unbuttoning his tuxedo jacket. Arliss had been expecting her to be nervous, and maybe she was, but it seemed like she was more excited. He made no objection as she undid his tie, unbuttoned his shirt, and ran her hands over her him.

Then she took his face in her hands, making him look her in the eyes. "All of you listen to me. I'm not a pastor right now. I'm a wife loving her husband for the first time. So please just make love to me the way you would if I was some other woman."

He put his hands over hers. "Honey, we will make love to you differently because we've never been in love before, and this means so much more than just the physical part. We want to show you how much we love you and how beautiful and exciting you are to us. But you're right; you're our woman and we're your men. Nothing else matters right now but that."

She smiled and kissed him as she helped him get the shirt off. It amazed her that despite how powerfully he was built that he could be so gentle. His muscles jumped a little when she touched his chest and she heard his swift intake of breath. The heat inside of him spread through her at the contact and she pulled him to her, kissing him hard.

Arliss growled as he encircled her waist with one arm and swept up her legs with the other. Her laughter broke their kiss.

"What are you doing?"

"Taking you to our little hideaway," he said, carrying her into the bedroom.

She let out a gasp when she saw the brand new, four-poster bed with a red silk canopy and side curtains. "What did you do?"

"We wanted to treat you like a queen, love," R.J. said. "Because you're the queen of our heart." He frowned as he put her down. "That didn't sound quite so corny in my mind."

She giggled. "I love the idea of being the queen of your heart. You're the king of mine."

R.J. laughed. "That really is corny, but you're right; it fits, doesn't it? Turn around."

She did and he slowly released the stays of her dress, brushing his fingers over her skin as he moved lower. Her shiver pleased him. Slowly, he undressed her, kissing her neck and caressing her long curves ever so gently. Her beauty was exhilarating, and it was difficult for him to hold back.

When they were bare, R.J. took her in his arms, kissing her tenderly, stoking the flames that were already building.

"How does this work?" she asked.

"What do you mean?"

Andi became a little flustered. "Uh, do you each—"

R.J. said, "No. This will be a little new for us, too. Whenever we've been with someone in the past, it was always one or another, but never all of us present at one time. We've never allowed it because they weren't the right person to experience it with. They weren't you, the woman who knows about us all, who accepts us and who loves us."

She smiled. "I hate the thought of you being with other women, but I love that I'll be the only one whoever gets to experience that with you."

"We'll never give you cause to mistrust us, love."

"I know."

Andi wrapped her arms around his neck, and kissed him hungrily. He responded in kind, and it was the kind of kiss where she sensed all of them at one time. In her mind, she saw all of the things they were thinking and it was thrilling. He backed her over to the bed and laid down with her.

It was a magical night for them, filled with sizzling passion and tender love. There were times when Andi felt like she was caught up in a firestorm of desire and pleasure and other times, carried along on a gentle current of love. She'd never imagined that making love would be like that, and she knew that it wouldn't have been with any other man.

Arliss gave himself to Andi completely on that night, letting her in the way he'd never done with anyone else. He, R.J., and Blake blended seamlessly, and there was no way to tell one from the other as he loved Andi. She made him whole, and gave him joy unlike anything he'd ever felt.

By the time their hunger was finally satisfied, Andi was pleasantly worn out. Blake took control. He gathered her to him and pulled the covers over them. "Rest, honey," he said. "Get your strength back because you're gonna need it after a while."

She looked at him. "I am?"

"Yep. We've been waiting a long time and that just whet our appetite for more. It was worth the wait, though. I'll say that," he told her.

She giggled. "You seemed to enjoy yourselves, I guess."

"No guessin' about it. It was … incredible. We've never felt anything so powerful before. I'm just warnin' you; we'll never get enough of you, so you'd better keep up your strength."

"Maybe you'll have to keep up your strength. I've been waiting, too, you know. I want to have a baby as soon as possible, so consider yourselves warned."

"We're all for that."

Andi stifled a yawn against his chest, and he settled her more firmly against him. "Sleep, honey. We love you."

"I love you, too," she murmured before succumbing to fatigue.

Blake smiled and closed his eyes, letting himself drop off into a contented slumber while he held the woman they loved.

Chapter Eleven

Gino went to the Express office to see if a telegram had come in from Father Carini in Billings. He'd been their family priest ever since they'd moved to Echo. They wished there was a Catholic church closer, and hoped that maybe someday there would be.

Molly looked up from her typewriter. "Hi, Gino. How are you?"

"Fine, thanks. How about you?"

"I'm good. How can I help you?"

"I'm looking for a telegram," he said.

"Oh. Go on over and see if Dan has anything for you," she said, smiling.

"Ok. Thanks."

He went through the door with the sign for the telegraph office. It needed to be somewhere away from the printing press so that Dan could properly hear it. When he entered the office, Dan was in the middle of copying down an incoming message. Gino waited patiently until he was done.

"Oh, hi, Gino," Dan said. He kept his blond hair cut short, because he had two cowlicks and longer hair never laid neatly. As it was, his hair tended to be spiky and unruly. It was appealing, though.

"Hi. Did you get a telegram for me?" Gino asked, smiling.

"Yeah. It's right here," Dan said, handing it to him.

GOOD TO HEAR FROM YOU. STOP. I REGRET TO INFORM YOU THAT THERE ARE NO MORE WEDDING SPOTS AVAILABLE THIS YEAR. STOP. FATHER REAGAN IN HELENA MAY HAVE SOMETHING. STOP. SAY HELLO TO YOUR FAMILY. STOP. GOD BLESS. END.

Gino wanted to crush the telegram, but he curbed his anger. "Thanks, Dan. I appreciate it."

"Sure, Gino." Dan kept the contents of the telegrams secret, but he couldn't help feeling bad whenever an unpleasant message came through. "I'm sorry," he said, his green eyes filled with sympathy.

Gino nodded. "It's ok. We'll figure out something. Will you please send a telegram to Father Reagan, asking him if he has anything available?"

"Sure. I'll do it right away."

"Thanks, Dan. I'll check back tomorrow," Gino said.

"Ok." Dan went to back to work, and Gino left the office.

He arrived home the following afternoon in a foul mood and found Alfredo in the tack room.

"Pop, I don't know what to do," he said.

"About what?" Alfredo asked.

"Father Reagan doesn't have any openings this year, either. I don't want to wait until next year to marry Carrie."

Alfredo sat down in the old overstuffed, leather chair in one corner. He'd been cleaning tack, and the scent of saddle soap filled the room. He returned to cleaning a bridle as he pondered the problem. After a couple of minutes, he sighed and stopped again. "Well, you've got two choices; wait until next year or have Andi marry you kids."

Gino passed a hand over his face. "Well, Andi did a great job with Sal and Lulu's wedding. I'll see what Carrie wants to do, but I don't see any other option. The problem is that there aren't enough Catholic churches around. Maybe someday we'll get a chapel here."

Alfredo said, "That would be great."

"Yeah. No sense wishin'. It could be worse," Gino said. "Ok, I'm goin' to check on those steer in the west pasture to make sure they didn't get through that patch I put on the fence. I'll see you at supper."

He left and Alfredo smiled. That was Gino. Out of all their boys, he complained the least. Sal ranted about things for a long time. Nick voiced his displeasure and then stewed, but Gino had a unique ability to just let things go. Alfredo did the same thing whenever possible, feeling that it was pointless to worry about something that couldn't be changed. It was better to concentrate on what he could change instead of driving himself crazy, he mused as he went back to work.

Carrie and Gino strode along by one of the pastures that night, holding hands. He'd just told her about Father Reagan's lack of availability and was waiting for her response.

It didn't make sense to Carrie for them to travel to another Catholic church further afield, because they wouldn't be able to attend all of the counseling meetings that preceded a wedding. Feeling Gino's strong hand wrapped around hers, Carrie experienced a peace that she hadn't in quite a while.

It had been only two weeks since they'd become engaged, but it felt longer. They shared so many interests and had similar outlooks on life. They did argue sometimes, but it ended up being more exciting than aggravating. Their anger never lasted long, and they often ended up laughing about it.

She loved the way he played with Fi, even capitulating the one night when she'd asked him to play paper dolls with her. Seeing the big, handsome man sitting on the floor with her, trying to put the paper clothes on the dolls was highly entertaining and they'd all laughed about his clumsiness.

A giggle escaped her, drawing Gino's attention.

"This is serious, Carrie," he said.

"Don't be grouchy. I know it is. I was just thinking about you playing paper dolls with Fi."

Gino laughed. "I can't help it my hands are too big to fold those little flaps over the right way. I tried, but they don't stay."

"You were so cute about it, and very sweet for going along with her. Not every man would. You're so good with her. Thank you for that," she said.

"You're welcome. She's too cute to resist." He shook her hand a little. "So what do you think about the issue at hand?"

"Well, I think under the circumstances, having Pastor Andi marry us is the best option, don't you?"

"Yeah, I do. Her and Arliss will be back from their honeymoon soon, and we can ask her then," he said. "Andi's pretty open-minded, and her and Nick are good friends. I'll bet she'll let us put some Catholic elements in the ceremony."

"I'm sure she will. We can have Nick help us with that. I know he's not a priest, but he was a seminarian, so he's knowledgeable," she said.

"Right."

They grew more excited the longer they talked about it, and decided to go see if Nick was busy so they could start planning. When they went in the house, they found the family gathered around the dining room table playing rummy.

Fi was laughing at something Sal had said to her. "You're just mad 'cause you're losing," she said.

Sal frowned. "Not for long, I'm not."

Lulu had more energy now, and she was playing for a little while. Serena slept in a bassinette close to the table. The baby didn't mind the noise, and hadn't woken up when Lulu had brought her out from their bedroom.

She said, "You're the most competitive person I know."

Sal grinned. "I can't help it. I don't know why."

Fi said, "Well, you're not winning tonight."

"Oh, yeah?" Sal said. "We'll see about that."

Fi narrowed her blue eyes at him. "I guess we will."

The family laughed at them. Gino and Carrie told the family their decision to be wed in Echo and everyone approved.

"Nick, can we talk to you for a little bit?" Gino asked.

"Sure," he said, rising.

They went to the Lion's Den, and spent the next hour going over the wedding. When they were done, they were happy with what they'd come up with.

Nick said, "I don't think anything will offend Andi, but she'll let you know if she approves or not."

They thanked him for his help, and then Gino took Carrie and Fi home for the night.

The next morning, Arrow was pleasantly woken by his wife, who was in an amorous mood. She'd been doing that more often lately, but Arrow was far from displeased. Her hand moved over his muscular chest, and she nibbled his earlobe, making him smile.

"Good morning," he said.

"Good morning. Did I wake you?" she asked, giggling.

He rolled over to her. "Yes, but I don't mind."

"Good," she said before kissing him insistently.

Arrow groaned and ran his hand up her thigh. Suddenly, Vanna jerked, breaking the kiss abruptly.

"What's wrong?" Arrow asked, looking into her wide eyes.

"I think my stomach growled, but it didn't quite feel like that. It was lower."

"Did it hurt?"

She shook her head. "No. It just felt strange. Oh! It just did it again."

Arrow pressed a hand lightly against her lower abdomen. "Right here?"

"Yeah. I don't feel sick or anything."

He pressed a little harder and felt a fluttering sensation under his palm. He gave Vanna a sharp look.

"What is it?" she asked, frightened. "What's wrong with me?"

"I think you're pregnant and you must be at least five moons along if there's movement," he said.

"Pregnant? I can't be pregnant! I haven't had any of the symptoms. No morning sickness, I'm not tired, I'm not irritable and I've had a few monthlies. They've been a lot lighter, but I've still had them," she said.

Arrow nodded. "I know, but not all women have those symptoms. They have other ones, like wanting to make love more often."

Vanna smiled. "That's just because you're so handsome and exciting. I think about you all the time, even when I'm at work." She put a hand over her mouth for a moment. "I have wanted to more, haven't I? I mean I always do, but lately it's been almost constant."

His laughter filled their room, and then he felt movement under his hand again. "Vanna, I'm sure of it. We've made an Italian Indian baby."

Vanna put her hand next to his on her stomach and the fluttering sensation reoccurred. Tears sprang into her eyes. "Arrow! We made a baby!"

They hugged, laughing and crying with joy, before their embrace turned passionate and they embarked on a sensual yet tender celebration.

Andi sat in her robe at the kitchen table in their little carriage house watching Blake make breakfast, while he wore only his underwear. Usually, he was the naughtiest of the three men, but R.J. had shocked her one morning by wearing only an apron while he cooked. She hadn't realized it when she'd first come into the kitchen.

She'd kissed him and sat at the table while he'd poured her a cup of coffee. She'd choked on it when he'd turned around, his bare tush meeting her gaze. He'd laughed at her shock even while she'd scolded him. She'd informed R.J. that he wasn't going to sit on the chairs naked.

He'd said, "Of course not, love. My bum will stick to the wood. It won't feel good at all when I stand up."

Now, as she listened to Blake argue with R.J. over how the eggs should be cooked, she giggled thinking about it.

Blake put a plate in front of her. "What are you laughing about?"

She gave him a wicked smile. "Naked cooking."

He laughed. "You want us to do that again?"

Her eyes glittered with amusement. "Maybe."

"There's a little devil in our angel, huh?" Blake said, kissing her. "Eat your eggs before they get cold."

She saluted him. "Yes, sir!"

Now that she was married to Arliss, it was perfectly acceptable to thoroughly enjoy the physical aspect of their relationship. Blake fixed a plate and sat down with her.

"Your dad did a great job of keeping things going for you. Of course, he's been doing this a long time, so that only makes sense. Are you excited about going back to work today?"

"Yes, I am. I know I'll have paperwork to catch up on, but that's all right. What are you going to do?"

"I'm gonna check in with the Indian school. I'll annoy Zeb for a while."

The captain wasn't fond of Arliss and his brothers.

"Be nice," Andi said. "He's doing a good job."

"I know. Between him and Cade, we don't have to do much. We wouldn't harass him if he didn't act like he had a stick shoved up his—"

"Blake."

Her warning tone stopped him. "Well, it's the truth. He thinks he knows everything and that his word is law. Anyway, when I'm done there, I'll head over to Lucky's and see if he needs any help today."

Being with her men full-time was a wonderful experience. They'd made love almost every night, which was extraordinary itself, but they also held her, making her feel safe and loved. They took turns slumbering with her, but Arliss was usually back in control by morning, because his consciousness was the one that liked being up early. Blake preferred to sleep longer, and R.J. was happy to get up early or sleep in if he had the chance.

Eating breakfast with them, and talking about the day ahead made her so happy. She'd been looking forward to sharing their lives and it excited her that they were now. They finished their meal and cleaned up before going to get dressed.

Blake and company had no qualms about being naked in front of her, but she was still shy about it because she'd never had a man see her that way. They knew this, and sometimes made certain to avert their attention from her until she put her chemise on so she didn't feel quite so uncomfortable. However, Blake wasn't ready to get dressed yet that morning. He embraced her when she took her robe and nightgown off.

"There's no real hurry, is there?" he asked, kissing her neck.

She shuddered as heat spread through her body. "No, I guess not."

"I was hoping you'd say that."

He kissed her, and the rest of the world ceased to exist.

Chapter Twelve

Later that day, Andi sat in her office with Gino and Carrie discussing their wedding. She understood their dilemma and was willing to perform the ceremony for them.

Gino said, "I hope you don't mind, but we have a few things we'd like to include in the ceremony."

"All right. Do you have a list?"

Carrie took a piece of paper from her purse and handed it to her. "If there's anything you're not comfortable with, just say so."

"I will," Andi said, looking over the list. "I don't see anything that would present any problem, though. I think they can be worked into the service. I see Nick is doing your readings for you. Very nice."

"Can I ask you a question?" Gino asked.

"Certainly."

"Does it bother you that he sings in the choir and comes to church, but he won't renounce his faith?"

Andi chuckled. "Why should it? He's a Christian, after all. I don't really care what denomination a person comes from. In the Salvation Army, I ministered to people from all walks of life, countries, religious beliefs, and races. Jews, Catholics, Hindu, Islam—all sorts. Most religions are very similar in that they have a supreme being and that they preach love and peace. That he feels comfortable enough to come is a great blessing to me and to the congregation, and it's a blessing to him, too. So it's a good thing all the way around."

Gino's brow furrowed. "Don't you want him and Maura to become members, though?"

"You mean do I want him to be put down on the official roll?"

"Yeah."

"I'd love that, but I know that none of you will ever change your membership from Father Carini's church and I don't expect you to. I don't poach parishioners. Some pastors and priests, do, but I don't play games like that," Andi said. "Any and all are welcome here at any time, whether or not they become an official member. If you come through that door and sit in a pew, you're a member as far as I'm concerned. That's what people of the cloth are supposed to do; welcome everyone the way Jesus did, not pick and choose who can and can't come."

Gino nodded. "That's good to know."

Carrie said, "I think it's wonderful to see a woman pastor. I know that there won't ever be female priests, but I think it's great that you have the opportunity to serve in the capacity you do."

"Thank you. Me, too."

Gino said, "We can't thank you enough for doing this for us."

"I'm happy to," Andi said. "Let's meet in a week so you can tell me how your plans are progressing to make sure everything is on track for March 28th."

They set up an appointment time before the couple left, and Andi looked forward to performing the ceremony.

Fi sat on a stone bench outside the school at recess that day. She watched the other children wistfully as they ran about playing, wishing desperately that she could play ball or take a turn on the rope swing. Suddenly, a boy a few years older than her came up and snatched away her crutches.

"Give those back!" she protested. "I need them."

"I just want to see them," he said, but his nasty smile said otherwise.

"They're too small for you, Calvin. You'll break them," she said angrily. "I'm telling Adam."

Calvin said, "How are you gonna do that? He just went inside. You can't walk to go get him."

"Give them back!" she shouted.

Otto appeared by her side. "Calvin, you give those back to her or I'll make you sorry."

Calvin smirked. "And what are you gonna do, half-breed? You're not as big as I am."

"I don't need to be," he said. "Now, give Fi her crutches back."

He advanced on Calvin, holding out his hand for the crutches, his dark eyes never leaving his opponent's.

"You want 'em? Fine, I'll give them to you," Calvin said.

He swung the crutches at Otto like they were a baseball bat. Otto neatly dodged them and rushed Calvin, ramming him in the stomach with his shoulder, and knocking Calvin to the ground. Calvin's breath left him in a big whoosh as his back hit the ground hard, and the fall dislodged the crutches from his grasp.

Although Otto wanted to hit Calvin, he didn't. He'd accomplished what he'd set out to do; retrieve Fi's crutches, and he didn't need to exert anymore violence than he already had. He got to his feet, picked up her crutches, and gave them back to her as Adam came over.

"What happened?" he asked, picking Calvin up off the ground.

Calvin's breath returned and he said, "He attacked me."

Adam looked at Otto, whom he knew well since he was friends with the Quinns. "Why did you do that?"

Fi said, "Calvin took my crutches and wouldn't give them back. He was mean and tried to hit Otto with them. Otto got them back for me. He just knocked him down. He didn't do anything wrong."

"Is that what happened?" Adam asked Otto.

"Yeah. I didn't hit him or anything."

Adam looked at Calvin with a serious expression. "You will not take anything from someone else that doesn't belong to you, and you're not going to hit people, either. You're not going outside for recess the rest of the week."

"Adam," Calvin protested.

"You heard me," Adam said. "Now go on back inside. Recess is over."

Calvin ran away, muttering to himself.

"Otto, you should have come to get me," Adam said. "It was nice of you to help Fi, but you can't go around attacking people, ok? I'm sorry, but no recess for you, either."

"I want to go to the Indian school," Otto said in a tight voice.

Adam's eyebrows rose. "Why? Don't you like school here?"

Otto said, "Because they don't call me half-breed there, and they don't punish you for doing the right thing!"

He ran away, not to the schoolhouse, but out of the schoolyard and across the road.

"Otto! Otto! Come back here!" Adam shouted. He would have chased the boy, but he couldn't leave the other children.

Otto kept going and soon disappeared from sight. Adam knew that Otto would get home safely, but he would go out to the sheep farm right after school to make sure he was all right. He'd hated to punish Otto, but he couldn't play favorites and he didn't want any fighting on school grounds. Sighing, Adam rounded up the rest of the kids and took them inside.

Carrie and Fi were having dinner with Gino's family that night. They all noticed that she was quiet and that she wasn't interested in eating. She'd been that way ever since Carrie had picked her up from school.

Carrie put a hand on her shoulder. "Sweetie, what's wrong. Don't you feel well?"

Fi put her fork down and rested her hands in her lap, but she didn't answer. Her eyes welled, and tears spilled from her eyes. Carrie put her arms around Fi and hugged her close.

"Fi, what is it? I can't help you if you don't tell me," she said stroking her hair.

"I don't want to be different anymore," Fi said.

Carrie sighed. Adam had told her what had happened at school, and had apologized profusely about it. "I know what happened today made you sad, but you can't worry about what other people think. You're a wonderful girl, and you have a bunch of people who care about you here."

"But I can't walk! I was stuck on that bench, Mommy!" Fi said, looking at her now. "What happens if there's no one around to help me?"

Carrie wasn't sure what to tell her, because it could happen. As independent as she wanted Fi to be, she realized that her daughter was more vulnerable than other children. "This is the first time anything like this has happened, Fi. I doubt there will be any more trouble with Calvin. It's going to be all right."

"Maybe not, but I still can't play tag or run with the other kids. It's not fair, Mommy. And Otto got in trouble, because he helped me and he probably won't want to be my friend anymore."

"Oh, honey, he'll still want to be your friend. What happened wasn't your fault," Carrie told her.

"No, he won't. All because of this stupid leg," she said, hitting her thigh.

"Fi! Stop that!" Carrie got hold of her hand. "You'll hurt yourself."

Fi struggled against her. "No, I won't. I can't feel much."

The girl became overwrought, breaking Carrie's grasp. She grabbed her crutches and left the table, heading towards the parlor as she started sobbing. Carrie would have followed her, but Alfredo beat her to it. He scooped Fi up and carried her into the parlor, sitting on the sofa with her on his lap. He rocked her and rubbed her back while she cried, murmuring to her in Italian.

His comforting presence, the motion, and the foreign language had a soothing effect on Fi and her sobs subsided into little hiccups. He gave her his handkerchief.

"Now, dry those pretty eyes of yours and listen to Nonno," he said.

She did and blew her nose. "Nonno? What's that?"

"That means grandfather in Italian."

"But you're not my grandfather," Fi said, confused.

"Sure I am. Your mommy is marrying Gino. He'll be your stepfather and that makes me your step-grandfather. But we're just gonna forget the step part of it, ok? So from now on, I'm your Nonno."

"Nonno," Fi repeated with a little smile.

"Good. Fi, your mommy is a smart woman. She was right when she said that you can't listen to the bad things people say about you. They're not worth your time. I'm not sayin' it won't bother you some, but don't let it get you so upset."

"But I hate my leg, because it doesn't work," Fi said. "I can't play like other kids do."

"I know what that's like," Alfredo said. "A couple of years ago, I had a heart attack, and I was real sick. I couldn't do any of the things I used to, and I didn't know if I would ever be able to again. It took a long time for me to get better and get back to work. There are still some things I have to be careful about."

"Like what?"

"Well, I can't help with the hay baling now, and I have to watch how much heavy stuff I lift. And I have to watch workin' outside when it's real hot in the summer. I have to take little breaks and drink enough water. And I have to keep my weight down some, which is hard because of the way your Nonna and Uncle Nicky cook."

"Nonna?"

"Grandmother. Sylvia. Fi, I know you're upset over your leg, but you were a very sick little girl and you have to give your leg time to heal. It's still sick, but it might get better, at least some. And if it doesn't, you find other ways of doing things."

"But I can't kick a ball or run, Nonno."

"How do you know you can't kick a ball?" Alfredo asked. Her usage of the grandfatherly term made him happy. It was the first time a child had called him that, and it made him feel good.

"I can't stand on one foot and kick with the other one," Fi said.

"You stand on one leg all the time. You can move your other one, right?"

"Yeah, but not hard enough to kick," she said.

"Have you tried?" he asked.

"Nonno, don't tease me." Her eyes became sad again.

"I'm not. I'm trying to show you something. Come here."

He stood her up and made sure she had her crutches. "Gino! Come here!"

There was no need to shout, because everyone had crowded around the parlor door to hear what he was going to say to Fi.

"I'm right here, Pop."

Alfredo saw all of them and frowned. "You all know better than to eavesdrop. Shame on you. Well, you might as well come here."

Gino asked, "What do you want me to do?"

Alfredo grabbed a small round throw pillow from the sofa and said, "You stand with Fi and make sure she doesn't fall. I'm gonna throw this to you, Fi, and you kick with that leg as hard as you can. Don't worry if the pillow doesn't go real far. It's your first try, but don't give up. Ok?"

Fi became excited, her usual fearlessness asserting itself. "Ok."

"Here goes. We'll see how good I can pitch," Alfredo said.

He tossed the pillow and Fi swung her bad leg at it. She was surprised when her foot hit the pillow and knocked it a little ways.

"I did it!" she yelled.

Everyone cheered and Carrie hugged her. "Yes, you did. I'm so proud of you."

Fi hugged her back and said, "Do it again, Nonno."

For the next fifteen minutes, Alfredo tossed the pillow to her, and Fi concentrated hard on swinging her foot. Most of the time it connected with the pillow. It didn't go far, but that didn't matter to Fi. She was amazed that she was doing it at all. The family cheered her on until she grew tired and called it quits.

Embracing her, Carrie said, "I'm so proud of you, honey. That was wonderful."

"Thank you. I'm sorry I got mad at you, Mommy."

"It's ok. I understand."

Alfredo took advantage of the opportunity he had, and while Sal's attention was diverted, he threw the pillow, hitting Sal squarely on the head.

"Hey! I didn't do anything," Sal said.

Alfredo laughed. "Not right now, but give it time and I'm sure you will."

Sal picked up the pillow and flung it back at him.

"Stop it!" Sylvia said. "You're gonna break something!"

Arrow snuck behind her and hit her on the rear with another throw pillow.

Suddenly everyone tried to get a throw pillow and a fight began, accompanied by a lot of laughing and exclamations of surprise. Vanna stood back with Carrie and Fi, but Sal wasn't about to let his little sister get away unscathed. He got her from behind and then grabbed her in a bear hug.

"Gotcha!"

Vanna giggled, but said, "Sally, don't."

"Oh no. You're no better than the rest," he said.

"Sally, stop!" she said, more insistently.

"Stop being a spoil sport," he teased her.

"Stop! I'm expecting!" she yelled.

Everyone froze where they were, and it was a humorous tableau as arms were poised to either throw a pillow or hit someone with one.

"For cryin' out loud, Noodle! Why didn't you tell us?" Sal said, gently hugging his sister. "I could have hurt you or the baby without meanin' to."

Alfredo whacked Arrow in the back of the head with the pillow he held. "Why didn't you say something? She coulda been hurt!"

"I didn't know he was going to do that!" Arrow protested.

Vanna couldn't help laughing at her husband, whose long, black hair literally stuck straight out all over his head from static electricity.

He looked at her. "Why are you laughing?"

"Your hair," she managed to get out before being overcome by laughter.

They all noticed and laughed at him. He looked at himself in a decorative mirror on the wall and laughed with them. Then they all gathered around the parents-to-be, congratulating them.

"We didn't say anything until I went to see Erin today," Vanna said. "We'll have our baby sometime in June."

Maura hugged her. "I'm so happy for you. You made a little Italian Indian."

The family laughed as they put the pillows back and straightened the room again. They all helped clear away dinner, and Carrie helped with the dishes. When they were finished, she went to get Fi around so Gino could take them home. She found her sound asleep, nestled against Gino's side.

Gino smiled at her. "We tuckered her out."

She sat down in one of the chairs. "She had so much fun. So did I."

He said, "You never know what's gonna happen around here."

Just as she was about to answer, someone knocked on the front door. Alfredo rose and went to answer it. "Lucky, c'mon in."

"Thanks, but I'm lookin' for Otto. Have ya seen him?" Lucky asked, his gray eyes frantic. "He didn't come home today."

"No, he hasn't been here," Alfredo said.

Lucky dragged a hand through his hair. "We've been lookin' ever since Adam came to tell us he ran away from the school. He's not at the Indian school or the Earnests'. Wild Wind and Roxie haven't seen him. He's not at any of our friends' houses. Evan's got Billy's dog out lookin' and Thad has Killer tryin' to find him, too. The trail from where Adam saw him disappearin' got lost at a creek a ways in from the road. He knows all the tricks for coverin' his tracks and stayin' hidden. That's the problem. And if he's been in the water with it so cold, I'm scared he'll run into frostbite."

Alfredo said, "Come in a minute. We'll come help you. Arrow's here. I'm sure he can help."

Lucky stepped into the foyer, grateful for a few moments of warmth. Soon the Terranova men were ready to join Lucky, who had been greeted by the women, and were all worried about Otto.

Gino got Carrie off alone. "Fi is still asleep and I don't know when we'll be back. Why don't you just stay here tonight? We have plenty of guest rooms."

Carrie looked at Fi and hated to wake her up, dragging her back out into the cold night. It wasn't as though there weren't other people in the house. "Ok. If you're sure it's all right."

"Of course it is. I'll carry her up for you," Gino said.

Gently, he gathered Fi in his arms and took her upstairs. He stopped at one of the empty rooms and had Carrie open the door.

"I'm sorry that it's cold in here," he said, laying Fi on the bed once Carrie turned it down.

"It's all right. I can get a fire going," she said, noticing that there was wood in the grate and that a box of matches sat on the mantle. "Don't worry about us. I hope you find Otto very soon. He's only Fi's age, and he shouldn't be out on such a cold night."

Gino nodded. "Ok. I'll see you in the morning for breakfast."

She grabbed his coat when he moved to leave. "Wake me when you get back, so I know if you found him. I doubt I'll sleep much anyway, knowing he's out there."

Since they'd been going out to the sheep farm for Fi's riding lessons, she'd become very fond of Otto, Mia, and Lily.

"Ok," Gino said.

Quickly, he pressed a kiss to her mouth before going out the door. Carrie smiled as she took off Fi's shoes and covered her up. She was making a fire when Sylvia came into the room.

"I'm so glad that you're staying," she said. "It's so cold. I just hope they find poor Otto quickly. He's been having a rough couple of years, I guess, from what Arrow said."

"What do you mean?"

"Well, he's just not sure where he fits in sometimes, because his biological mother is Cheyenne, and he was raised on a reservation until he was almost four. Come downstairs once she's all settled, and we'll tell you about it. I don't think she's gonna wake up anytime soon. I put some coffee on and we have some coffeecake," Sylvia said.

"All right. I'll be down shortly," she said, smiling.

Sylvia went over to Fi and kissed her forehead. "She's such a dear girl. I know this has to be hard on the both of you, but you're not alone anymore. You have people you can count on, Carrie."

Carrie held back the tears that burned her eyes. "Thank you so much. You don't know how much that means to me—to us."

Sylvia said, "I remember when we first moved here and didn't know anyone. We were so happy when we started making some friends. I know how it feels to be in a strange place with no one else you know. Things will be all right from now on."

As Sylvia left the room, Carrie had a warm feeling inside and sent a prayer of gratitude heavenward for the wonderful people she'd met—especially a handsome, Italian cowboy with big blue eyes and an even bigger heart.

Chapter Thirteen

As Gino rode and walked through the woods and fields, hunting for Otto, he thought about Carrie and Fi. He was glad that he'd kept relatively calm about the situation and had gotten the chance to get to know Carrie. She was an incredible woman, and he was happy about their upcoming wedding.

He'd tried to control himself around her, but it was hard when she incited such passion in him. Her kisses were so sweet, and she felt so good in his arms that he never wanted to stop. But, he didn't want their relationship to be just about passion. Nick and Maura had stepped over that line very quickly. They'd barely known each other before succumbing to desire. Of course, Nick had still been drinking heavily back then, and his judgment had been compromised.

Sal and Lulu had also been physical before marrying. Gino didn't judge either of them for it, but he'd learned from them. Sal and Lulu had almost broken up for good shortly before their wedding. He hated to think that she might have gone back to New York, possibly carrying Sal's child. Nick and Maura had also been lucky in that regard. They, too, had had difficulties before marrying and if she'd gotten pregnant, the baby would have possibly been born out of wedlock.

Gino didn't pretend to be an angel, but he hadn't been with nearly as many women as Sal had been. After Sal had won the bet of who would get married first, and he hadn't gotten any interesting letters, Gino had given up on the idea of a mail-order bride. Then he'd been passed over by Chelsea, who had preferred Nick, and he'd gotten soured on the idea of trying to find a wife at all. Around Christmas, Alfredo had urged him to try again, so he'd put in another ad. He didn't know if he loved Carrie yet, but he desired her, he respected her, and she was a wonderful mother. A man could certainly do worse for a wife. And then there was Fi. He adored the little girl and wanted to provide for her.

Although they looked for hours, the search party didn't find Otto, and eventually they had to call it quits so they could get warm again and get something to eat. If Otto didn't show up by dawn, they would resume the search. When Gino got home, he found Sylvia, Vanna, Maura, and Carrie dozing in the parlor.

He smiled at the cozy picture all of the sleeping women made. Going over to Carrie, he bent and kissed her forehead. Her eyes fluttered open.

"Gino? Where am I? Oh, my goodness. I fell asleep down here. I didn't mean to," she said getting up. "Did you find Otto?"

The other women heard them and also woke.

Gino shook his head, his expression grave. "No. We looked everywhere."

Carrie said, "Oh no. I'm sure Lucky and Leah are frantic."

"Yeah, we tried to get him to go home, but he won't. We're all gonna get a little rest and head back out on fresh horses once it's daylight."

The rest of the men came into the house, and hung up their coats. Sylvia went to put more coffee on, but the men all said they were ready for a little shuteye, so she didn't bother. Carrie checked on Fi and was relieved that her daughter was still sleeping. She stirred the embers in the fireplace and put more wood on once the flames were high enough.

Lying down on the bed with Fi, she prayed for Otto's safe return. She'd only been sleeping for about two hours when Fi woke her up.

"Mommy, I have to go," she said.

"All right," she said, giving Fi her crutches and helping her. When that was accomplished, she asked Fi, "Honey, do you know of somewhere Otto might go? Did he ever mention something to you?"

"Why?"

"He hasn't come home yet. They've been looking everywhere for him," Carrie said.

Fi's eyes widened. "He hasn't?"

"No."

Fi's brow knitted in concentration. "Oh! He said something about a knot the one day, but I didn't understand what he meant. Maybe he went there."

"A knot?"

"Yeah."

It didn't make sense to Carrie, but maybe it would to the others. She and Fi freshened up and then went downstairs to see if the men were up now that the sun was up. She hoped that they hadn't missed them. Luck was with her. When she and Fi entered the dining room, they greeted all those gathered.

"Fi said that Otto once mentioned something about a knot to her as somewhere he might go. Does that mean anything to you?"

Sal asked, "Did he say the Devil's Knot, Fi?"

"Yeah. That was it. The Devil's Knot. He goes there sometimes."

The men all got up.

"Sal, you go over to the sheep farm and see if Lucky is there. The rest of us will go to the Devil's Knot and look around for him," Alfredo said. He kissed Fi's forehead. "Good girl."

"Thanks, Nonno. Bring him home."

He smiled and they all left.

"That's the last of the caves," Win said, dropping back to the valley floor of the cave-pocked canyon. "He's not in them and there's no sign of a fire or anything."

Win used to live in the caves during the summer months before he'd met Lucky. He knew them intimately and was good at climbing the rock walls.

"Damn it!" Lucky said. "When we find him, I'm gonna spank him until his bottom is red."

Wild Wind had come along with them. "Lucky, I think it's time you rested. You can't keep going like this. We'll find him."

"We've looked everywhere," Lucky said. "Where else could he be? What if he's lyin' hurt somewhere or what if—"

"Don't think like that, Lucky." Wild Wind put a hand on his shoulder. "Otto's a smart boy. He'll be fine. Let's go home and get a little rest."

Lucky forced himself to be reasonable. "Aye. A little rest will be good."

The sound of a horse coming in their direction attracted their attention. Marvin rode up to them, his eyes wide with alarm. "Lucky, this telegram came in just a little while ago."

Lucky took it from him.

MA AND DA DON'T WORRY ABOUT ME. STOP. I'LL BE FINE. STOP. I'M GOING WHERE I'LL BE WANTED. STOP. I LOVE EVERYONE AND I'LL SEE YOU AGAIN SOMEDAY. STOP. LOVE OTTO.

"It came from Dickensville," Marvin said. "What does he mean by that?"

Lucky grew very pale. "He's goin' to find Avasa. At least he thinks he will. She sent him a letter a couple of months ago. I didn't know he was so unhappy that he'd run away." Despite his strong effort, Lucky couldn't hold back the sob that shook him. Fatigue and heartache brought him to his knees and he let out his misery as he knelt on the ground.

Wild Wind crouched next to him and hugged him. "It will be all right, brother. We'll go get him."

Lucky nodded and straightened, pushing up onto his feet again. "Yer damn right we will. I'm going to get Thad and Arliss. Will you watch the sheep farm for me, Wild Wind?"

"Yes," Wild Wind said.

"Thanks. Oh, Lord. How the hell am I gonna tell Leah?" He wiped away his tears and took a couple of deep breaths to clear his head. Wild Wind watched Lucky roll his shoulders the way he always did when preparing for battle. "I'll tell her, and then I'm goin' to get our son back. I waited too long to have him, and I'm not gonna lose him again."

"Lucky, I'll ask Thad to meet you at your house," Marvin said. "And if I see Arliss, I'll do the same. Do you really think Otto will get far?"

"Marvin, he's not like other boys his age. He's been trained by warriors how to fight and evade enemies. He's good at huntin' and fishin', too. He knows how and where to make a camp and how to make a fire," Lucky said. "So even if he hasn't got any money, he knows how to survive."

"But he's only eight," Marvin said.

"Tell that to the man he helped kill a couple of years ago when he came lookin' for Arliss," Lucky said. With that, he strode to his horse, mounted, and rode away.

Carrie had taken Fi back to their room at the Hanovers' to change her dress before taking her to school. She'd been afraid that Fi would balk at going and was glad that she didn't. Then she went back to the boarding house to gather up clothing to wash in the Hanovers' laundry room.

As she worked, she kept praying for Otto to be found. Once the clothes were washed, she hung them on the lines that Arthur had hung in the large room. It was much better than hanging them outside where they would freeze and then need to be warmed again. Finished, she got around and headed for the store, wanting to get some more of Fi's peaches.

"Carrie!"

She turned at the sound of Gino's voice and smiled as he rode up. "Hello? Any news?"

He dismounted and came over to her. "Yeah, but not the kind you want to hear," he said and told her about Otto's telegram and that Lucky and his friends were going after him.

She was shocked. "Oh, poor Lucky and Leah."

"Yeah. They'll find him," Gino said. "They're all talented at this sort of thing, and Lucky isn't the kind of guy to give up, either. Are you busy? If not, come to the diner and have some coffee with me."

Carrie said, "I'd like that. I can't believe he was that upset that he ran away."

As they entered the diner, Gino said, "The way Wild Wind talked, he thinks it's been coming on for a while. You know about Otto helping to save his family from the guy who came after Arliss. Lucky and Leah were proud of him, but at the same time, he can't go around throwing knives at people. The same as he can't knock people down all the time. He's only doing what he's been taught how to do, but he doesn't understand when it's ok and when it's not.

"It's not Adam's fault. He was only doing his job, but when he punished Otto, I guess it was the last straw. Otto wants to go find Avasa and live with whatever tribe she's with. If they're still free. Thad took her to find them, so he knows where they are. I'm sure they'll find him."

"I hate the thought of him being out there all on his own. He's just a little boy, regardless of what kind of training he's had," Carrie said.

"I know," Gino replied.

They ordered their coffee and had a piece of apple pie with it. When they left, Gino walked with her to the boarding house and went in with her. He wanted to talk to her about something, but he hadn't wanted to do it in public. When she entered the parlor, she stopped so abruptly that Gino bumped into her from behind.

"Connor," she said faintly. "What are you doing here?"

A man of average height with dark hair and blue eyes rose from the sofa, smiling at Carrie. "Well, Glory be. I'm glad I found ya, Carrie."

Gino surmised by his Irish brogue that he must be some relative of Carrie's late husband. He also sensed that Carrie was not pleased to see him. She pressed her back against Gino, who put his hands on her shoulders in a protective gesture.

"You shouldn't have come here," she said.

The tension in her shoulders transferred to Gino, putting him on edge.

"Well, I've come to honor my commitment to ya," Connor said.

"What commitment?" Gino asked.

Connor met his gaze. "Carrie and I were supposed to be married, but she ran off with Fi before the weddin'."

Carrie felt Gino jerk a little in reaction and she closed her eyes.

Connor's eyes moved between her and Gino. "And who would you be, sir?" he asked.

"I'm Gino Terranova, her fiancé."

Connor smiled genially. "Connor Sheehan, Carrie's brother-in-law." He held out a hand to Gino who shook it. "I'm sorry to tell ya, but Carrie will be comin' back to Chicago with me so we can be married."

"No, I will not be, and I'll never marry you," Carrie said. "I'm marrying Gino and there's nothing you can do to stop me."

"Oh? Isn't there now? I picked Fi up already. If ya want yer girl, ye'll come with me," Connor replied.

"How dare you?" Carrie said, going right up to him. "You give my daughter back right now. Where is she? I'll send the sheriff after you if you try to leave with her."

Connor gave her a patronizing smile. "For his sake, I hope ya don't."

Gino said, "Don't underestimate our law enforcement, Connor. Kidnapping is a serious crime."

"Look, mate, I don't have any quarrel with ye, but if ya stick yer nose into this, I will, and ya don't want that," Connor said.

"Seeing's how I'm her fiancé, it does involve me. So consider my nose stuck into it."

Connor ignored him. "Carrie, be at that Burgundy House place by three o'clock today to go back. We'll be leavin' whether ya come or not."

Gino moved towards him, but Connor pulled a gun from a coat pocket. "Ya don't wanna do that, lad. If ya want Fi, ye'll be there, Carrie. Three o'clock. Don't involve the sheriff. I'm not alone. Chaz and the others are with me."

Carrie's hands clenched in anger and fear as Connor moved past her and left. Gino spun her around, making her let out a cry of surprise. He gripped her upper arms tightly.

"What the hell is goin' on, Carrie? Start talkin' and don't leave anything out this time." His fury-filled eyes bored into hers.

Sorrow, pain, and fear mingled inside her and she had to swallow hard, so she could speak. "I was an accountant for the Irish mob in Chicago. Aidan was as trapped as I was. They made him run booze and whatever else. I don't know, because he wouldn't tell me. I'd gone to business school, which you knew, and they made me falsify their books.

"Both of us wanted out, especially when Fi came along. We started saving money, so that we could disappear, but they must have suspected because—" Her voice cracked. "Because he didn't come home one night and then Connor came to tell me that he'd been found dead in an alley, shot by a mugger. I didn't believe him, but for Fi's sake, I acted like I did. If they'd have thought that I suspected the truth, they'd have killed me, and I didn't want her raised by them.

"So I played dumb and went through the motions, but I loved Aidan so much and I truly mourned him. In their family, it's traditional that when a man who has a family dies, an unmarried brother will marry the widow and help raise any children she has. Connor was forcing me to marry him. Then Fi got sick, and I had to play along with him again, so that she could be taken care of. But once she was getting better, I found your ad and started writing you and then it worked out, so I grabbed what money I had and we came here. That's all of it, I swear."

She trembled in his hands and the terror in her eyes was the kind that was hard to fake. Gino had never wanted to perpetrate violence against a woman, but he wanted to shake her right at that moment. He released her arms to avoid the temptation. "I don't believe you. You've lied to me and my family at every turn. How am I supposed to believe anything you say?"

She grabbed his coat. "Don't you understand how desperate I was? I had three choices; marry him, be killed or run. I chose running. I know how this looks, but I've come to care for you so much, and I never thought he'd find me here. I don't know how he did. I never contacted anyone from there or told anyone where we were going. I'm telling you the absolute truth. I swear to God I am. I swear on Fi that I am. Please help me, if only for her sake, Gino. Once I have her back, we'll leave again—"

"Oh, no, you won't. We'll get her back and get married. I'm not gonna leave Fi unprotected," Gino said. "There's only one thing that men like Connor understand: money. I'm gonna pay him off. You stay right here until I come back for you this evening. I'll get Fi back." He walked to the front door and stopped. "I sure have bad luck with women. I don't find one to suit me and then I think I might have, but she doesn't want anything to do with me. Then you come here and ... I fell in love with you. I fell in love with a liar and manipulator. I sure know how to pick 'em. Stay here."

He opened the door and went out, slamming it behind him. Carrie stood rooted to the spot. *He loves me?* The joy she felt was soon wiped away by heavy guilt, and her heart constricted painfully. She sat in a chair before she fell down and put her head in her hands as she burst into tears.

Chapter Fourteen

"This has been a hell of a couple of days," Alfredo said. "Where is Carrie now?"

"She's at the boarding house," Gino said.

He'd explained what was happening to the family members who were at home. "I just can't wrap my mind around all of this. I'm so stupid. I never shoulda trusted her after she sprang Fi on me like she did. I'd have still had her come if I'd known about her. I know that now."

Alfredo said, "I'm glad to hear that. Fi's the one we have to think about right now."

"I know," Gino said. "We're gonna pay Connor off so he'll leave and never bother her—or us—again. I'm gonna go to the Burgundy House and make a deal with him."

"Not alone you're not," Sal said. "I'll go with you."

Alfredo said, "I'm gonna go get Carrie. She'll come stay here for now, until you figure things out."

"There's nothin' to figure out, Pop. We're still gettin' married, for Fi's sake. I'll do it for her," Gino said. "I shoulda never put another ad in the paper. I knew it was a mistake. And now look, I'm in love with someone I'll never be able to trust and be bound to her for life. Let's go, Sal."

With angry strides, he left the Lion's Den.

"He blames me for pushin' him to put that ad in," Alfredo said.

"It ain't your fault that she lied."

Alfredo said, "I didn't say anything to him because he's too angry and hurt right now to hear it, but I've had some experience with both the Irish and Italian crime families and I don't blame her for doin' what she did. They don't let you out once you're in, Sal. I'll be she didn't know until after her and Aidan were married, and then it was too late to do anything about it. She ran because she was desperate."

Sal sighed. "Yeah. It's a hell of a situation to find yourself in. And so is Gino's. I didn't know he'd fallen in love with her."

"Gino holds some things close to the vest. He must have been planning to tell her when he thought it was right," Alfredo said.

"Sal!" Gino shouted.

"Comin'!" Sal hollered back.

Alfredo followed him out to the kitchen where Gino waited impatiently. The three men were quiet as they left, each intent on their mission.

Carrie couldn't believe it when Alfredo showed up.

"Gino told you," she said.

"Yeah. Let's get your things together," he said. "You're stayin' with us now. It's too dangerous for you to stay here alone."

She shook her head. "No. I won't do that to you. I've brought more than enough trouble to you. You must hate me."

"Sit down with me," Alfredo said. They settled on the sofa. "Carrie, one of the reasons that Sylvia and I moved out here with the kids was because I had a cousin in the Italian mafia who was pressurin' me into getting involved with them. I know how they operate and I didn't want that for myself or my family. I could never lead that kind of life. I ain't exactly happy with what you did, but I understand. I don't hate you, Carrie. But from here on out, you're gonna have to be completely honest with us."

Carrie nodded as tears of remorse slid down her cheeks. "I will be. I promise. I don't deserve your help or sympathy. I did it for Fi, Alfredo. I couldn't let her grow up in that kind of environment."

Alfredo understood. "I know. Do you love Gino?"

Her smile was watery. "I do. I never thought I'd meet anyone like him. He's such a wonderful man, and I love him for all that he is." Her smile faded. "But it doesn't matter. He told me he loved me before he left today, but I'm sure that love will die because of this. He's right to distrust me. You all are. I don't even know why you'd want to be bothered with me."

"Because I know that you were between a rock and a hard place. I'd do anything to protect my family, so I get why you did it. I also love that little girl, and I'll do anything to protect her, too," Alfredo replied. "Now, you get your things together. I'll be back in a bit."

"I'll never be able to repay you," Carrie said.

Alfredo hugged her. "You just be good to Gino. That'll be repayment enough."

She nodded against his shoulder. "I will."

He let her go and left, promising to return shortly. Carrie dried her tears and went upstairs to pack. As she did, resolve to make it all up to Gino filled her. She would be the best wife she could be to him, and made a silent vow to work hard to regain his trust.

Evan and Shadow listened to Alfredo's story without interrupting him. When he was done, a smile spread over the handsome sheriff's face. He looked at Shadow. "Would you like to become famous for helping to bring down some of the Irish mafia?"

Shadow grinned. "I'd love to. What did you have in mind?"

"Here's how it's gonna go ..." Evan began.

While they were concocting a plan, Gino and Sal walked into the Burgundy House, which was now owned by the Earnest brothers, and greeted the former owner, Kevin, who had stayed on as their manager.

"Hi, fellas. What can I get you?" he asked.

They noticed a man wearing guns sitting behind the bar. He regarded the Terranovas suspiciously.

Gino said to the stranger, "I'm here to see Connor. I'm Gino Terranova."

"Ya weren't supposed to come. Carrie's s'posed to be here at three," the man said, standing up.

"We have a proposition for Connor," Gino said. "Tell him it's worth his time to listen."

After a moment, the man said, "All right. I'll go see what he says."

He went up the steps to one of the rooms that used to be rented out to prostitutes. In a few minutes, he came out and called down to them. "He'll see ya. Come then."

Sal and Gino went upstairs to the room the man had indicated. Connor sat at a table inside.

"Hello, lads. So ya wanna do some business. What kind?" he asked.

The brothers sat in a couple of chairs.

Gino said, "I'm gonna make it worth your while to go away and leave Carrie and Fi alone for good."

Connor cocked his head a little. "Keep goin'."

"I'll pay you ten thousand dollars cash, which I can have by three today. But then you have to go and never come back. Just forget they ever existed. If you do come back, I won't be so nice," Gino said.

"Ye must really love her if yer willin' to pay that much," Connor said. He mulled it over. He didn't love Carrie that way. He liked her well enough and he liked Fi, but he didn't really want to take her on. However, he took his familial obligations seriously, and out of respect for his brother, he'd been determined to marry Carrie and take care of Fi. He saw a way to be rid of the both of them and make some serious money. "All right. Ya get me the money by three and we'll disappear for good."

Gino held out his hand. "Do I have your word of honor on that?"

Connor was a believer in a code of honor in his own way. "Aye. Ya do," he said, shaking Gino's hand firmly.

The brothers rose.

"We'll be back by three," Gino said.

Sal and Gino wasted no time in leaving and heading for the bank.

Lucky, Thad, and Arliss rode towards Helena, asking about Otto along the way. No one had seen him, however. Instead of becoming disheartened, determination burned brighter inside of Lucky every time they received a negative answer. He was going to find his boy no matter what, no matter how long he had to search, he'd bring him home.

Thad and Arliss had never seen Lucky like that before. His face wore a hard expression most of the time now and a powerful resolve filled his gray eyes. At one point he stopped.

"We're not gonna find him this way. He knows to stay away from people. He's goin' through the woods. Most likely followin' a stream. That's what I'd do if I were him."

Thad said, "There was a stream a ways back on the right side of the road."

Lucky said, "Let's see if we can find it and work our way back. Traveling through the woods takes longer and he's not on a horse, either, so we might be able to head him off."

They cut into the woods on the right, riding for about fifteen minutes before coming across the stream. As they rode back the way they'd come, Lucky prayed that they found his son before any harm befell him.

Chapter Fifteen

"Now, all you have to do is go in there and give them the money," Evan said. "While you're in there, try to find out how many of them there are, so we know how many of us it's gonna take to catch the rest of them, ok?"

Gino nodded. "Ok. I'll do anything to get Fi back."

"I know," Evan said. "We'll get your girl back."

He took a breath and said, "I better get in there. It's almost three."

Evan patted his shoulder and Gino and Sal rode the rest of the way up to the Burgundy House. He didn't know how many people Evan and Shadow had with them, but they were apparently in position already. They could have stormed the place, but Evan needed evidence of extortion and kidnapping. Connor had to actually take the money to constitute extortion. That's where the Terranovas came in.

Entering the establishment, Gino nodded to Kevin, who looked nervous. Connor sat at a back table with a couple of men. The one he'd seen earlier was sitting behind the bar once again. He couldn't see any other henchmen, but that didn't mean that there weren't more upstairs.

"Well, nice to see ya again, Gino. Come sit down," Connor said.

They each took a chair, and Gino handed him a pair of saddlebags. "It's all there. Where's Fi?"

"I'm gonna count it if ya don't mind," Connor said. "It's not that I don't trust ya, but I don't. Know what I mean?"

Sal had a hard time keeping his mouth shut, but he didn't want to do anything to anger Connor, so he restrained himself.

The wait while Connor double checked the money was excruciating. Gino wanted to get Fi back and get out of there.

Connor finished and said, "Yer a man of your word, Gino. I'm glad to see it. Liam, go get the girl."

One of the men sitting with them went upstairs and entered one of the rooms. In a few moments, he came back out, carrying Fi, who was crying.

"I want Mommy. Where is she?"

Gino was off his chair as soon as heard her. "Fi? Fi!" He ran up the stairs and took her from Liam.

Fi wrapped her arms around his neck, sobbing.

"Shh, sweetheart," Gino said in Italian, remembering how it had soothed her before. "It's all right. You're safe now."

Sal was on his feet. "Remember, you forget you ever knew Carrie and Fi and don't come back here. You got your money, so the deal is done. Agreed?"

Connor nodded. "Agreed. I'm a man of my word, too."

Sal just nodded and walked with Gino out the door. It was hard not to run to their horses, but that would have looked suspicious. They mounted and trotted away, meeting up with Evan around a curve in the road that was out of sight of the bar.

"There were only four of them that we saw, but I don't know if there were more upstairs or not. One of them is behind the bar with Kevin. The poor guy is a nervous wreck," Gino said.

Evan said, "I'm glad you got your girl. We'll take care of Kevin. Thanks, fellas. You did your part and you did great. Go on home. I'll get your money back to you."

They bid the sheriff goodbye and took off for home. Evan rode to the meeting place where Shadow and a few others waited for him.

"They only saw four, but there might be more. Shadow, take off your badge," Evan said, removing his.

"Why?" Shadow asked, but did as Evan wanted.

"Because you, me, Win, and Keith are going in there for a good time. We're just some buddies having a few drinks. The rest of you split up and cover the exits. If you hear a ruckus, get in there. I've already deputized you, so if you kill one of them, that's ok," Evan said. "Everyone ready?"

They all nodded.

"Ok. Let's go."

Connor and his buddies watched Evan and company came through the door, laughing and talking noisily.

"Gents, we're closed at the moment," he said. "Come back later."

Evan looked at Kevin. "You're closed? But your door is open. You never close this early. We want to buy my buddy, Keith, a few drinks. It's his birthday today. Set 'em up, Kevin."

Connor got up. "I don't think you heard me. I said we're closed."

Evan looked at him. "Do you own the place now? Did you buy it from Kevin?"

"Something like that. Now, go find somewhere else to drink," Connor said, resting his hand on his gun.

A loud bray sounded from outside the front door, and Win almost groaned. He should've known that Sugar would find a way to follow him.

"What the heck is that?" Connor asked.

Win said, "I'm sorry. It's my burro. She follows me everywhere."

"Burro, eh? I'll bet she's cute."

Evan latched onto an idea. "Win, go bring her in so they can see her. She does tricks. Kevin, you don't mind, right?"

"No, go right ahead." He was so relieved to see them that he didn't care what they did.

Win went to the door and opened it. Sugar and Basco trotted inside and began inspecting the place. It was a funny thing how even criminals have a soft spot for animals. Win introduced the burros to Connor and his men. Then he started putting them through their routine of tricks. The man who was behind the bar came out to see them, too, which was what Evan had been hoping for. Shadow motioned for Kevin to take cover and the bartender dropped down to the floor quickly.

Basco decided it was time to mark his territory and peed on the floor, which sent everyone into fits of laughter. At a signal from Evan, he and his men made their move on Connor and his associates while they were busy laughing at Basco. They drew their weapons.

"Hold it right where you are," Evan said. "I'm the sheriff and we're taking you in for kidnapping and extortion. Give yourselves up peacefully. Don't make me shoot you."

Shadow said, "Let them fight us. I haven't had the pleasure of shooting anyone lately. I'm overdue."

Win said, "He's a little trigger happy, so I'd behave if I were you."

Connor grabbed Sugar around the neck. "You're gonna leave here or I'll put a bullet through her brain."

Win snickered, which turned into a full belly laugh. "I've been trying to get rid of her, so you'd be doin' me a favor." He laughed the way he knew irritated Sugar, who hated to be made fun of.

Her tail started switching back and forth and she grunted. Win laughed again, and she squealed, trying to get away from Connor, who hung onto her. Evan took the opening and shot Connor in the leg. Connor shouted in pain and fell to the floor. Outraged at this point, Sugar kicked Connor in the ribs. One of the other men made a run for it and Shadow calmly drew a bead on him and squeezed off a shot. Although it would have given him great pleasure to kill the man, he'd only fired a warning shot. It slammed into the floor near the man's feet.

"If you want to live, stop where you are. If you don't, and I would be glad if you didn't, keep running."

The man stopped and put up his hands. Shadow handcuffed him. Evan had done the same with Connor, hauling him to his feet. Sugar kept trying to get at him, so Win got her and Basco out of the place.

"Kevin, sorry about the burro pee," Win said, grabbing one of the other men.

Kevin stood back up. "Don't worry about it. I'm just glad to be alive."

Evan said, "I'm gonna have to have Leah make a deputy vest for Sugar, too. She comes in handy."

Win grinned and shoved one of the criminals towards the door. They filed outside with them, Keith practically dragging the injured Connor out the door.

"Wait until the guys in prison hear that you were taken down by some country lawmen and a couple of burros," Evan said to Connor. "You mafia boys aren't so tough after all."

Connor glared at Evan before Keith helped him mount a horse. Evan and his men just laughed at them as they mounted up and headed for the sheriff's office.

Fi recovered quickly from her ordeal. Although she'd been frightened, no harm had come to her. She'd just wanted to see her mother. Once she'd been safely riding home with Gino, her buoyant personality had resurfaced. Gino was greatly relieved that she hadn't been hurt in any way. He kept hugging her as she sat in front of him and telling her that all was now well.

Sal watched Gino with her and smiled. His brother's love for Fi was evident in his determination to get her back and his relief that they had. He was acting as any good father would. Gino, blinked back tears a couple of times as they rode as he thought about what might have happened to Fi. He thanked God that she was safe with him now.

Gino knew that he would have been devastated if Carrie and Fi had left. He didn't know what was going to happen with Carrie and him, but he couldn't deny that he loved her. He also loved Fi and he would have been devastated if they'd have left.

When they arrived home, the front door opened and Carrie ran for them. She must have watching for them.

"Fi!" she cried upon seeing her daughter. "Oh, Fi!"

She reached up for Fi and Gino handed her down.

"Mommy, I missed you," Fi said. "I was scared they wouldn't let me see you again."

Carrie stroked her hair. "I'd have come for you. Don't you worry about that. You're all right now and no one's ever going to take you again. Let's get you something to eat." She looked up at Gino. "Thank you both so much for everything you did."

Gino gave her a tight smile and rode on to the barn, Sal following him.

The rest of the family except Lulu had joined them outside now, and Alfredo carried Fi inside. Fi's crutches had been left behind at the Burgundy House, but Gino was planning on going back for them once they knew the coast was clear. Sylvia insisted on fixing a snack for everyone. Once they were finished, Carrie took Fi upstairs to lay down for a little while. As she watched Fi sleep, Carrie's mind drifted to Gino. She owed him so much, and even though she had no idea how, she would find a way to repay him.

Gino came back from retrieving Fi's crutches that night and found Carrie in the barn petting the horses when he got back. He knew she'd been waiting for him and frowned. He wasn't sure he was ready to talk to her.

"I know you're angry with me, Gino," she said when he dismounted.

"You're damn right I am."

"You have every right to be, but please try to see my side of the situation. I was all alone with a little girl. There was no one I could truly trust, and I was being forced to commit crimes. I could have gone to prison or been killed and then Fi would have been all alone," Carrie said.

Gino remained silent as he took his horse into its stall and removed its tack. Then he brushed the horse down and put the tack away.

Carrie came into the tack room and shut the door. "Aren't you going to say anything?"

"There's plenty I could say, but I don't think you wanna hear it." His eyes shone with anger in the light from the lamp she'd lit in there while waiting for him. "Like how if you had told me in your letters the kind of trouble you were in, I would have helped you."

"How was I to know that?" she asked. "I didn't know you from Adam and I was supposed to tell you that I'd unwittingly married into a crime family, and I had a little girl and wanted out?"

"Yes! At least I would've known and I could've made an informed decision! As it was, I had Fi sprung on me. I would've accepted her if I'd have known about her beforehand. My letters should have told you that much. Then, a bunch of mob guys come here after you. At least if I'd have known about them, I could've been on the lookout or something.

"We could've warned Adam not to let Fi go anywhere with anyone strange and told her not to, either! I was scared to death that Connor would hurt her, or that you'd both go with him!"

"I know it's all my fault, Gino. I accept the blame for it," Carrie said.

"Is anything about you real?" His eyes locked on hers. "You said you came to care for me, but is that just a lie? I need to know the truth, Carrie. If you have an ounce of feeling in your heart for me, tell me the truth." His frustration and anger was so hot that he grabbed her and shook her a little. "Tell me the truth!"

"Yes! My feelings for you are real, Gino. I never expected to fall in love with you, but I have. That's the truth. I swear!"

He saw it in her tearful eyes, and even in his anger, his heart filled with happiness. However, he didn't smile, he growled and brought his mouth down on hers as his emotions sought release in action. She didn't resist him, instead wrapping her arms around his neck and pulling him closer.

Gino kissed her harder and thrust his hands into her hair as a groan of need escaped him. Her ardor matched his, and then she whimpered in surprise as he broke the kiss and pulled back from her. "Go up to the house right now."

"What? Why?"

His jaw clenched. "Because if you don't, I'm going to take you right now, and it wouldn't be right. I need to calm down before we talk about this anymore."

The intense passion in his eyes was exciting, and she knew that he was right. Her emotions were as high as his were, and she needed to clear her head, too. Without another word, she left the barn, hurrying to the house.

I should have known that Father would find me, Otto thought as he rounded the bend in the stream and saw Lucky sitting by a fire. Looking at the position of Lucky's little camp, he saw that Lucky had set up there purposely because it was set back from the stream far enough that someone coming along wouldn't see it until they were out in the open.

Lucky looked up from the fire, staring into his son's eyes. His instinct was to grab him, hug him, and then spank him, but refrained from doing any of that. Instead, he said, "Well, there ya are, lad. I was gettin' worried about ya."

Otto considered his options, and he knew that running was pointless because Lucky would just catch him and drag him home. If he was going home, he was going to do it with his head held high. He sighed in resignation and went to the fire, sitting across it from Lucky.

"Hello, Da," he said.

"Hello. Did ya have a nice trip then?" Lucky saw that although Otto was dirty, he didn't look like he'd sustained any injuries and he was greatly relieved.

"I was having a nice trip."

Lucky smiled. "Until I showed up, right?"

"Yes."

"Yer a very resourceful and smart boy, Otto, but whether ya like it or not, ya are still a boy. I know ye've been confused, but yer ma and I can't help ya if ya don't talk to us," Lucky said.

"You don't understand, Da, and you never will," Otto said.

"Again, I can't unless ya talk to me."

"I'm called half-breed and all sorts of things when Adam isn't around and sometimes by grownups. No one calls you that because you're not an Indian. You don't know what it's like! I don't say anything because there's no point. It won't change anything."

"Well, I know it's sort of different, but I'm Irish and a lot of people don't like the Irish. I've been called a mick, cat-lick, because I'm Catholic, drunk, and some other really nasty names I'm not gonna repeat. So I know what that's like. Ya can't let them get to ya. Ya can't run from them because they're anywhere ya go. Even if ya make it to Avasa, the people she's with might not like ya because of yer white blood. It works both ways. When I was with her tribe, I was always bein' challenged and discriminated against, but I didn't back down. I don't mean fightin' all the time. That doesn't work."

Otto said, "I don't fight all the time. I threw that knife because we were in danger. That's what a warrior is supposed to do."

"Aye, but Otto, yer tryin' to grow up too fast. Yer not a warrior and yer not an adult. As much as ye don't like it, ya hafta obey the rules. Adam has rules against fightin' and I know ya were helpin' Fiona, but ya could've really hurt Calvin. Do you know what that woulda done if ya had?"

"Showed him not to bother Fi or me again."

"Well, maybe, but it woulda also showed everyone they were right about yer Indian blood makin' ya a stupid savage. A good warrior stops to think about all possible outcomes before he acts. Ya didn't think about that angle, did ya?"

Grudgingly, Otto said, "No."

"And ya also didn't think what would happen once ya got to Canada. What if they're not there anymore? What if after she wrote you that letter, somethin' happened to her? Eventually, some adult would see ya and catch ya. They would put you in an orphanage somewhere and then what?" Lucky asked.

"I'd run away again."

"And go where? How long would ya keep runnin'? Is it so bad with me, yer ma, and all of the other people who love ya that ya had to run away? Don't ya love us?"

"Aye. I love all of you so much, but I don't know where I belong," Otto said.

"I do. Ya belong with all of us, and anyone who doesn't like ya can go jump. Ya just don't bother with those people, Otto. That's what I do. But I do owe ya an apology."

Otto was confused. "You do?"

"I do. Ya see, I didn't explain things to ya well enough. I shoulda told ya that the only time ya fight is when there's no other choice. If ya can't reason with someone and they're gonna hurt ya, then ya have the right to defend yerself. Or, if they're gonna hurt someone ya love. Now, I know yer thinkin' about that man who came after Arliss. We were in danger, but between us grownup men, we could've handled it.

"I would've preferred to take the man alive and get information from him. We mighta been able to do that. Of course, Arliss wasn't quite himself, and I think he reacted too fast. Otherwise, he would've just disarmed the man and conked him on the head."

"I didn't think about that," Otto said.

"I didn't expect ya to. Yer still learnin'. That's what I'm tryin' to tell ya. It's not that I'm not proud of ya for protectin' yer family, I'm just askin' ya to think things through and maybe leave some things to the grownups. It's gonna be the same thing if ya find yer mother. Ye'll have to listen to yer elders, and if ya do something that messes up a hunt or puts the tribe in danger because ya didn't listen to them, it won't go well for ya."

Otto nodded a little. "I see what you mean. You're takin' me home, aren't you?"

"Nope. Not if ya don't wanna go. Ya see, I'd sooner see ya happy somewhere else than miserable with me. I've loved ya ever since I knew Avasa was pregnant with ya, and I'll always love ya no matter what. But if I force ya to go home, ye'll just run off again if yer not happy. So the choice has to be yers. If ya wanna try to find yer mother, I'll take ya. If ya don't, we'll go home. Now, if ya come with me, yer gonna be expected to follow the rules, even if ya don't like them," Lucky said.

"You'd take me to find Mother?"

Lucky's heart hurt, but he said, "Aye. We'll stay here tonight. Ya can think about it and let me know in the morning which it'll be. For now, though, I roasted some pheasant. We'll eat and get some sleep."

Otto nodded and ate the food his father gave him, his mind working the whole time. Watching him surreptitiously, Lucky saw how much he'd misjudged Otto. There were some Indians, or even half Indians who couldn't fully adjust to mainstream society. Did that apply to Otto even though he was so young? Was his Cheyenne blood so strong within him that it canceled out his white blood and a new way of living?

It reminded Lucky of the way Wild Wind had chafed so badly when he'd been confined to the Earnests' lair last summer. If it was on his own terms, Wild Wind did just fine, but when he was cornered or held captive, he reverted to his Cheyenne nature. Maybe Otto was the same? But how could Otto live on his own terms when he was just a boy? Lucky held back a sigh as he turned the problem over in his mind. When it was time to sleep, he still had no solution and prayed for the Great Spirit to show him one.

Chapter Sixteen

Carrie had left Gino be the night before, knowing both of them needed time to regain their composure before talking again. After breakfast, Gino insisted on driving Fi to school. Once again, she'd been determined to go despite the events of the day before. Since it was Friday, Carrie had allowed her to go. Gino also wanted to get his money back from Evan and redeposit it.

Carrie had talked to Fi about not going with anyone trying to pick her up at school except for her or one of Gino's family members and she knew better now. When Gino dropped her off, Adam felt terrible, but he hadn't suspected anything odd about Connor since Fi had been so excited to see her uncle. Gino assured him that it wasn't his fault before going to get his money.

As he went about his business, Gino thought about the situation with him and Carrie. Trust was essential in any relationship or else there really wasn't one. He needed to be able to trust her, but could he? She'd said that he now knew everything and that she loved him. Her feelings had seemed so real the previous night. The rawness of the hunger in her kisses and her touch had been so powerful that he was sure she'd meant it. He needed to find out for sure, though, and headed his buggy for home to do just that.

Carrie wandered around the ranch, at loose ends since Fi was at school. She was just about to come inside when Alfredo opened the front door.

"Oh, good. There you are," he said. "Could you help me with something since Gino isn't here?"

"Of course," she said, following him into the Lion's Den.

Several ledgers lay open on the large conference table. Alfredo sat down and patted the chair next him.

"I'm puttin' your brain power to work for me. Something's not adding up here, but I can't figure out where I made a mistake. These are for the chicken operation, which Gino doesn't really look at a whole lot, since he's got his hands full with the beef side and some of our other investments," he explained. "A fresh pair of eyes would be great."

"I'd be happy to take a look," she said.

"Thanks. Ok. I'll leave you to it. You don't need me lookin' over your shoulder. I'll be in the greenhouse with Maura if you need anything," he said.

"Ok," Carrie said and got down to work.

That was where Gino found her when he got home.

"Hi. What's all this?" he asked, sitting down.

"Alfredo asked me to take a look at the chicken operation books because there were some discrepancies and he couldn't find them," she said. "I've found them and corrected them. Based on what I've found, there's actually more revenue coming in that he'd had figured."

He looked at her sharply. "There is? That's not like Pop. He's usually really careful about the books. He's had to be all these years. Show me."

Carrie walked him through everything she'd done, showing how she'd arrived at her conclusions and how she'd gotten there. Gino traced the dates back to a few months after Alfredo's heart attack, and he grew concerned. These weren't mistakes that Alfredo would normally have made. Was there something else going on with his father?

"Thanks for doing this," Gino said. "You untangling this is a big help."

He looked at her and then back at the ledgers. If Alfredo wasn't up to the challenge of this side of the business, he should have said so, but he knew how proud his father was. Doing something like that would be very difficult for him. Carrie was obviously a talented accountant. No wonder Aidan's family hadn't wanted her to get away.

"Carrie, I need to know some things," he said, looking her in the eyes. "Did you mean it last night when you said you love me?"

"Yes," she said without hesitation. Her heart beat faster. "I meant every word I said last night. I know you don't trust me, but I love you very much."

Gino said, "Well, after what you just did, I do trust you. You could've messed up these books or hidden money or any number of things, but you didn't. You figured it all out and put things to rights. I think why all of this hurt me so much is because I felt like you should have trusted me more. That's not exactly reasonable thinking on my part in a way. I put myself in your position last night after you left the barn. I sat there a long time thinking.

"Your choices were limited, and you did what you thought was best for Fi. I see that now. I don't like that you were in danger, and I don't like it that you couldn't trust me, but I understand. But, once you got here and you got to know me a little, why didn't you tell me?"

Carrie said, "Because I just wanted to forget about the past. I never thought they'd find me. I still don't know how they did. I just wanted to build a future with you and Fi, and whatever other children we have. I never meant to hurt you or bring danger to you. I'm so sorry, Gino. There's nothing else like that in my past, though. I promise and I'll always be truthful with you. I lied by omission, but everything I've ever told you has been the truth."

"I believe you," Gino said. She'd met his eyes and hadn't fidgeted at all. He saw regret in her eyes, too. "And I'm gonna hold you to that truthful part."

"I promise. Except when you ask me what I got you for Christmas or your birthday. Or presents in general. I'll never tell you what they are," she said, her eyes sparkling.

He smiled. "I guess I can deal with that. Now, I have a question for you."

"All right."

"How would you like a job?"

She laughed. "Is this another proposal?"

"No, it's a real job," he said, grinning. "I'll have to talk to my family about it, but how would you like to take over the bookwork for the chicken operation?"

She gaped at him. "You would trust me to do that?"

He motioned towards the ledgers. "Yeah. Look at what you just did. You know what you're doing and it would really help us."

"Won't your father be angry?" she asked. "I don't want to horn in on his work."

Gino said, "I'll talk to him. It'll be ok."

Carrie mulled it over. "If your family agrees, I'd love to help out."

He grinned. "Great. By the way, I really do love you. I'd hoped that we'd fall in love the way Sal and Lulu did, but I knew that might not happen. I'm sure glad it did. I know you're a good person, Carrie. I was just so mad and upset last night and I'm sorry if I hurt your feelings."

"You had every right to question me," Carrie responded. "I brought it on myself. I'm not angry at you. I'm glad you feel as though you can trust me now."

"I do." He gave her devilish smile. "I don't suppose you have your glasses on you."

"As a matter of fact, I do. It's force of habit to put them in my pocket in the morning."

"Put them on," Gino coaxed.

"Only if you speak Italian," she countered.

"Si tratta di una trattativa. ut loro il mio deserto fiore."

Gino still couldn't say why her glasses excited him so much, but it didn't matter. He was mesmerized as she too them out and slid them on, giving him a coquettish look once they were in place. "How do I look?"

"Siete la donna più bella che abbia mai visto e ti amo." he said.

The burning passion in his eyes and the beautiful way he spoke made her feel a little breathless. "What does that mean?"

"That you're the most beautiful woman I've ever seen and that I love you," he said, before claiming her lips.

Alfredo came down the hallway towards the open door of the Lion's Den, and saw them kissing. A smile spread across his face, and he turned around and left, happy that they'd apparently worked out their differences. He'd prayed for Gino to find happiness, and it looked like he had. They'd also gained another daughter and a granddaughter in the process. Yes, things were coming along nicely.

Epilogue

Earlier that morning, Lucky had woken Otto. "Time to be movin', lad. Which way are we goin'?"

Otto's dark eyes took on a mischievous gleam. "Well, I don't know which way yer goin', but I'm goin' home."

Lucky laughed at his impersonation of him and joy sang through him over Otto's choice. He grabbed the boy, hugging him tightly as tears stung his eyes. Otto hugged him back.

"I am sorry, Father," he said in Cheyenne. "I am sorry I hurt everyone. I will not run away again. I will face these people, and show them that I am better than they think I am."

Lucky let him go, cupping his little face in his hands. "You are better. Do not ever forget that. You are not a savage any more than you are a mick. You are Otto, my son, and I am proud of you. So many people love you and are proud of you. You are not alone."

Otto nodded. "Yes, Father."

"Good. Now, we must go. Thad and Arliss are waiting a ways up the trail," Lucky said. "I told them we would meet them there by nine."

"Uncle Thad and Arliss came with you?" Otto asked.

"Yes. They were worried about you, too," Lucky said as they broke camp.

Otto flashed a smile at Lucky. "Three men after one eight winter's old boy. I must be an even better warrior than I thought."

"Go on with ye," Lucky said, scowling as he switched back to English. "Get movin'."

"Aye, Da."

"What's going on down there?" Erin asked Lucky as she joined him and Leah on the porch of their house.

Leah signed. "As soon as Carrie and Fi arrived a little bit ago for her riding lesson, she started taking Otto to task for running away. It's been so funny watching them."

Out in the sheep pasture, Fi said, "I can't believe you would leave me like that."

"Leave you? What do you mean?" Otto asked.

"I thought we were friends."

"We are friends," he affirmed.

Fi said, "You don't leave your friends like that, Otto. I missed you."

"You did? I wasn't gone all that long," he said.

She shook her head. "It doesn't matter. I still missed you, and I feel like you wouldn't have run away if it wasn't for me. If you hadn't helped me, Adam wouldn't have punished you and made you mad. And you wouldn't have run away."

Otto rode Sugar over to Basco and made her stop. "It's not your fault, Fi. I wanted to help you and I'd do it again, too. I won't let anyone pick on you like that."

Her big blue eyes met his dark gaze. "Do you promise not to run away again like that?"

He drew himself up proudly. "I promise to never run away again."

She smiled at him. "Thank you. Race you!" She urged Basco into a canter and the two of them went across the meadow together, laughing and teasing each other while the adults looked on with smiles.

Fi's riding lessons had strengthened both of her legs and other muscles, too, and she could move even faster on her crutches. She was a good rider now and Gino was having Jerry Belker, the mayor make a harness like Basco's to fit on a pony he'd bought for Fi. Jerry was skilled at leather and wood working.

Fi now played kickball with the Terranovas almost every day and could kick the ball farther and swing around the bases on her crutches. They had fun with it, too, and they even convinced some of the ranch hands to play with them. Carrie and Fi were grateful for the kindness they'd been shown. The Terranovas were grateful for the chance to have Carrie and Fi in their lives. They were all blending together very well and creating lasting bonds.

Arthur proudly walked Carrie down the aisle behind Maura, her maid of honor, who followed Fi and Otto. Fi had balked about being the flower girl because she didn't want everyone looking at her while she moved along on her crutches. But Otto had insisted, telling her that if he wouldn't let other people's opinions bother him anymore, then she had to do the same.

So she'd agreed and Otto helped her by holding the flower basket for her. She stopped every little bit, took a handful of flowers and spread them. Her progress was a little slower, perhaps, but everyone was proud of her, especially Gino, who watched her with a wide smile.

Although she'd been a surprise to him, Gino was glad that she was here. He would see to it that she had everything she needed, but most of all love. He'd never imagined becoming a father that way, but she was so easy to love and he'd been overjoyed when she'd asked if she could call him Pop. He'd agreed instantly, hugging her tight.

He winked at her as she and Otto finished their part, and she smiled at him before sitting with her Nonno and Nonna. Looking back up the aisle at his bride, Gino's smile widened when he saw that Carrie was wearing her glasses.

The woman who seemed to float towards him in her cream colored dress with golden accents, had also been quite a surprise. In fact, their whole relationship had been full of surprises—some wonderful and some distressing—but they'd worked through them and come out on the other side.

It was also a surprise that he wasn't getting married in a Catholic church the way he's always envisioned, but at that moment, Gino didn't care. All that mattered was that he was marrying the woman he'd come to love and be forever joined with her. Carrie hadn't expected to find a man who would love Fi and show so much kindness towards her. And she certainly hadn't expected to fall in love with a tall, handsome, Italian cowboy with a big heart and a head for numbers.

As they joined hands, Gino whispered, "*Non ho potuto sognare una donna più bello e non vedo l'ora di fare l'amore con voi.*"

Carrie didn't know exactly what he'd just said, but she was sure that he'd just told her that she was beautiful. She would make him tell her later on, but Andi started the ceremony and there wasn't time.

As they exchanged their vows, Sylvia whispered into Alfredo's ear. "Finally a groom and not a best man."

He grinned. "Yeah, and he brought me an accountant, so I can just work in the garden and the greenhouse, too," he whispered back.

"You're so bad," she said, chuckling.

He smiled and their concentration returned to the ceremony. There was nothing wrong with his accounting skills at all. He'd purposely put some errors in the one ledger, so that he could test Carrie in the hopes that she was as skilled as he'd thought. That she was meant that he could concentrate on what he'd grown to love; growing produce for Nick's restaurant.

After his heart attack, working with the plants and soil had become a relaxing, enjoyable way to work and he liked contributing to the new venture. He would still keep a hand in their livestock operations, but for the most part, he was now free to doing what he liked. He'd confessed what he'd done when Gino had asked after his health. Gino had been angry with him for scaring him like that and then amused at Alfredo's craftiness.

Gino slid Carrie's ring on as he said, "With this ring, I thee wed." He felt a sense of completion, as though all of the pieces of his destiny were falling into place. As Carrie repeated the phrase to Gino, peace settled in her heart. Fear and uncertainty were replaced by happiness and a feeling of security.

Their first kiss as a married couple was filled with promise and a hint of passion as they embraced. The wedding guests clapped noisily as the newlyweds were presented and left the sanctuary.

It was the first time in the Terranova's history that a reception would be held in a saloon, but Gino and Carrie had surprised them with their venue selection. They'd had such a good time dancing there, that they wanted to experience it again as they started their married life. As they danced, they laughed and smiled into each other's eyes, their hearts joining.

Sylvia captured Gino and Carrie's attention during a slower dance, and pointed across the room. They looked and Carrie gasped and covered her mouth while Gino grinned. In a quieter spot, Otto and Fi danced. He'd had her stand up and put her hands on his shoulders while he'd laid her crutches on a nearby chair.

She held onto him and balanced on her good leg, as they swayed back and forth to the music. A bunch of people watched them, smiling and Leah had Dan take a few pictures of the adorable pair. Once the song was over, Otto gave Fi her crutches and they sat down, unaware of the attention being paid to them.

The Quinns came over to Gino and Carrie.

Lucky said, "Could be a sign of things to come."

Carrie said, "It's so sweet. You've raised a wonderful little boy, you two. I'm so glad you were able to find him and bring him home, Lucky."

"Me, too," Lucky said.

Leah said, "I was worried sick the whole time. I love him so much and I can't bear the thought of him not coming home."

Lucky put an arm around her. "Don't fret now, lass. He's home safe."

"I know," she said, resting her head against his chest.

Although he hadn't voiced his concerns to Leah, Lucky wondered if Otto's Cheyenne spirit would ever feel completely at home in Echo. Otto certainly seemed to be a peace there now, but a niggling doubt had settled at the back of the Irishman's mind. For now, though, he pushed it far down and just enjoyed watching the two youngsters interact.

Gino also watched from a father's perspective, but in a different vein than Lucky's musings. He hoped that Fi found someone to love and appreciate her when the time came, but for now, he wanted her to just be happy. He wanted her to know she was loved, and that she could always count on him. Although he didn't want to replace her father, Gino wanted to be important in her life and give her security.

It would be the first time Carrie had ever been away from Fi, but while she would miss her girl, she knew she was in the very best care and wasn't worried about going on her and Gino's honeymoon to Cheyenne. She knew that God must have guided her to find and answer Gino's ad. It had to be divine intervention for her to have found such a wonderful man and an equally wonderful family.

When they left that afternoon, the happy couple was given a loud send off, with a few rowdy comments hollered after them that made them laugh.

Along the way, they stopped at a beautiful hotel for their wedding night, planning to leave for Cheyenne again in the morning. Carrie was enchanted by the elegance of the Charlemagne Hotel and impressed with the attentive service.

"I've never stayed in a place like this," she said as they entered their room.

Gino put their bags down. "I don't often, but I wanted to do something special for you. It's not that I couldn't, but I never had anyone to share a fancy hotel room with before." He took her in his arms, caressing her cheek. "I plan on spoiling you, Mrs. Terranova."

A sweet smile curved her mouth. "I like the sound of that. I plan on spoiling you, too."

"Oh?" he asked. "How so?"

"I'll be by your side no matter what happens. You'll never have to question my loyalty to you, or whether I'm telling you the truth or not. I'll be your confidante, I'll cheer you up when you have a bad day, and I'll love you unconditionally."

He frowned, even though everything she'd just said pleased him greatly. "You just had to show me up. I was just gonna spoil you by buyin' you stuff."

She laughed. "Go right ahead, but that's not what matters to me."

"Well, I guess I can do all of that stuff for you, too," he said with mock reluctance.

"You can always spoil me by speaking Italian."

"And you can always spoil me by wearing those glasses."

"Well, I have them on, but I don't hear Italian coming out of your mouth."

Gino's eyes darkened with desire as he told her beautiful she was and how much she excited him. Their kisses were punctuated by words of love spoken in Italian and English, but mostly just allowed to speak for themselves as they undressed each other.

Her Italian cowboy's muscles enticed her to touch him and she no longer resisted the urge. His caresses and demanding kisses heated her body, and she lost track of everything but him.

Gino loved the way she smelled and the softness of her skin against his lips and hands. She excited him in ways that he'd never known and his desire for her was unquenchable. Their joining that night wasn't merely of the flesh, but also a union of hearts and minds. It was an expression of a love that would sustain them for the rest of their lives.

Start of a new story.

While the newlyweds were celebrating their new marriage, back home in Echo, the night was filled with a much less pleasant kind of drama.

Dog Star and Skyhawk had sneaked out after bedtime, as was their habit, and had been traversing the woods in back of the Burgundy House. They laughed and talked about their latest pranks on Captain Zeb Rawlins, one of the two army officers who'd been assigned to help protect the Indian school. They enjoyed aggravating him, seeing him as a representation of their enemy.

Dog Star's buckskin fringed leggings got caught on a branch. When he reached down to unsnag them, it wasn't a stick he touched. What he closed his hand around was distinctly human. He cried out and jumped back.

"What is it?" Skyhawk asked, coming to his side.

In the dark, the boys couldn't make out much more than a woman's form and eyes, but it was obvious that she was dead from her fixed, vacant stare.

"We have to get the sheriff," Dog Star said.

Skyhawk said, "I'll go to the bar and get help. They can send someone. We'll have to show them where she is. Don't touch her."

"Don't worry, I won't," Dog Star said, not liking the idea of being alone with the corpse.

Skyhawk ran off and Dog Star prayed that he would soon return.

When Evan arrived, Shadow was already there.

"Hello, boss," he said, smiling.

"Hi. You got here fast."

Shadow said, "Marvin and I were playing at the bar when Skyhawk came in."

"Oh. I'm glad. I'd hate for a bunch of people traipsing around here," Evan said. "What did you find so far?" Evan asked as he looked at the woman in the light from the lanterns Shadow had brought from the Burgundy House.

"Well, she was tied up at some point before she died. There are rope burns on her wrists and ankles. Her throat was slashed. I'm guessing she's been here about a week. Whoever killed her was in a hurry. They stuffed her partway under this log. Perhaps they were interrupted and didn't get her buried. There's also a curious mark on her upper thigh. More like a brand."

Using a stick, Shadow pulled the woman's skirt up, revealing her leg. The mark was in the shape crescent moon positioned like a backwards C that faced a single star. A chill stole over Evan.

"The Star of Lucifer," he said.

"An occult symbol?" Shadow asked.

"Yeah. It's also called Satan's Star."

Shadow asked, "What aren't you saying, Evan? I can tell that this means more to you than some random symbol."

Evan stood straight again. "It does. When we found Darlene Daughtry, she had a symbol just like this one on her upper thigh. I'll be able to tell better in the daylight, but I'm certain that this was carved by the same person."

Shadow said, "You never caught the murderer."

"No. We're gonna guard these woods tonight, Shadow. If there's one woman out here, there may be more. Those kids might have stumbled onto a dumping ground. We looked all through this area when Darlene was killed, but she might have been the first victim, which would explain why we never found anything."

Shadow nodded. "That's a distinct possibility. I'll go let Marvy know that I won't be going home tonight. He wanted to come with me, but I didn't want any more disturbance of the ground than necessary. Not that he would have, but—"

Evan's laughter interrupted him. "I'm finally starting to rub off on you. You're actually listening to me when I'm harping at you about procedure. I'm amazed."

Shadow chuckled. "Yes, but don't expect me to ever be completely tamed."

"Truthfully, I don't want you to be," Evan said. "Ok, go tell Marvin and ask him if he'll go get Thad for me. And have him swing by to let Erin know that we'll be bringing her at least one body to examine tomorrow."

"You would think that I was one of your deputies," Marvin said from a couple of yards away, surprising them.

Shadow said, "I told you to stay inside in case there was danger."

"Shadow, are you forgetting that I've been on a covert mission, fought dangerous adversaries, and survived to tell the tale? I'm not disturbing anything. Ask nicely, Evan, and I'll help you," Marvin said.

Evan's jaw clenched. There were still times when Marvin could be an ass, but it would be convenient if he didn't have to go do the errands. "Fine. Will you please help us out?"

Marvin smiled. "Very well. Do you want me to ask Dr. Wu to come aid you as well?"

Evan smiled back at him. "No. Since you're so eager to help, you come back after you're done with all of that and bring a gun with you. You're deputized, jackass. Now get a move on."

Shadow let out a bark of laughter and felt Marvin's cold anger in his mind. "You must admit that was rather ingenious, Marvy."

Marvin let out a Shadow-like growl and strode angrily away.

By the time eleven o'clock the next morning came, the final body count had reached six. All of the other five women had the same brand on their upper left thigh. Several men had helped with the removal of the women and they'd been taken off to the town hall, which had been closed down while it served as a temporary morgue.

Looking out over the six now-empty gravesites, Evan said, "Boys, we've got us a serial killer on our hands." He looked over at Shadow and did a double-take when he saw the glee-filled smile on Shadow's face. "What the hell are you so happy about?"

"I've never had the chance to catch a serial killer before," Shadow replied. "I look forward to the challenge."

"You mean other than yourself?" Thad quipped.

Evan's head quickly swiveled in his direction. "What do you mean?"

Thad's gaze locked on Shadow's. The sudden fear and rage he saw building in Shadow's eyes told him two things; Marvin had never told Shadow that Thad knew about their parents and that Shadow had never told Evan about any of it; how they'd murdered their parents or where they'd put the bodies.

Oh, hell, Thad thought. "Well, just look at him. Doesn't he look the part? He's got those spooky glasses and he mostly dresses in black," he said to cover his gaff.

Evan looked at Shadow who somehow managed to pull off a cocky smile when he wanted to pulverize Thad and Marvin instead.

Evan smiled. "Yeah, he does, but that's not what you meant at all, Thad. Don't pee on my leg and try to tell me it's raining out. I know you too well for you to be able to lie to me. Now, how about you two tell me what the hell is going on?"

Marvin had also heard the exchange and Shadow's fury burned inside his brain. This is not how he'd wanted Shadow to find out that he'd shown Shadow's cage to Thad. He knew what a sensitive subject it was for his twin and hadn't wanted to upset him.

Shadow turned towards Marvin and walked up to his brother, giving him a malevolent smile. "Why don't you explain it to the good sheriff, brother mine? You seem to be good at telling the tale."

"Shadow, please remain calm. Going off the deep end will solve nothing," Marvin said.

Shadow grabbed the front of Marvin's coat and shook him. "How could you do that to me? How could you tell? It wasn't your place!"

Marvin shoved back, not about to be pushed around. "Let me go! You think that it's only your story to tell? Who was there with you?"

"That may be so, but you didn't live down there—"

"Hey!" Evan yelled. "What's going on? Stop talking to each other and start talking to me!"

"No!" the twins said in unison.

"Ok, I'll just have Thad tell me, then," Evan said.

"Do not open your mouth, Thad," Shadow said.

Thad said, "Don't tell me what to do. I didn't know he hadn't told you and that you hadn't told Evan. It's been how long now. I don't understand what the big deal is anymore."

Shadow said, "I don't expect you to understand. I'll do my job, but I'm not discussing this anymore. Are we done here?"

Evan knew that he wasn't going to get anything out of Shadow right then. "Yeah. Sure. Go write up your report."

Shadow growled and stomped off without looking at Marvin again. Marvin glared at Evan and Thad and also left.

"Why are they mad at me when I'm the only one who doesn't know what's going on?" Evan asked.

Thad patted him on the shoulder. "Don't worry about it. It's nothin' you wanna hear anyway."

Evan batted his hand away. "Don't patronize me, Thad! I'm not a kid anymore. I'd like to know what's bothering my deputy and friend so much, and neither you nor Earnest will fill me in so I can help him."

"Evan, it's not my story to tell," Thad said. "It's theirs."

"Fine. I'm going home. Be at the clinic by three to hear what Erin found out. That's an order," Evan said.

"Who do you think you are?" Thad asked.

Evan didn't back down. "Right now I'm your boss, because that way I don't smack the crap out of you for keeping secrets from me."

"Jeez, Evan. You sound like a little kid who's been left out," Thad said.

Evan poked Thad's chest. "No, what I am is pissed, because I seem to be the only one who realizes that Shadow needs to get whatever this is off his chest. It seems like Marvin already has, although not to me. That's fine. I don't expect him to. He and I will never be friends again, but Shadow's different. Whatever it is, must be bad for all of you not to trust me. I can see why they wouldn't, but I never thought you'd ever distrust me, Thad."

Thad watched his best friend walk away with regret. "Me and my big mouth. I'm sorry, Evan, but I just can't tell you," he said to himself.

He whistled for Killer, and mounted up when the big stallion came to him. With a heavy heart, Thad rode home while somewhere in Echo, a new enemy waited to strike again.

The End

Thank you for reading and supporting my book and I hope you enjoyed it. Please will you do me a favor and leave a review so I'll know whether you liked it or not.

Linda's Other Books

Dawson Chronicles Series

Mistletoe Mayhem: Book 1

Echo Canyon Brides Series

Montana Rescue
(Echo Canyon brides Book 1)
Montana Bargain
(Echo Canyon brides Book 2)
Montana Adventure
(Echo Canyon brides Book 3)
Montana Luck
(Echo Canyon brides Book 4)
Montana Fire
(Echo Canyon brides Book 5)
Montana Hearts
(Echo Canyon brides Book 6)
Montana Hearts
(Echo Canyon brides Book 7)
Montana Orphan
(Echo Canyon brides Book 8)
Montana Surprise
(Echo Canyon Brides Book 9)

Montana Mail Order Brides Series

Westward Winds
(Montana Mail Order brides Book 1)
Westward Dance
(Montana Mail Order brides Book 2)
Westward Bound
(Montana Mail Order brides Book 3)
Westward Destiny
(Montana Mail Order brides Book 4)
Westward Fortune
(Montana Mail Order brides Book 5)

Westward Justice
(Montana Mail Order brides Book 6)
Westward Dreams
(Montana Mail Order brides Book 7)
Westward Holiday
(Montana Mail Order brides Book 8)
Westward Sunrise
(Montana Mail Order brides Book 9)
Westward Moon
(Montana Mail Order brides Book 10)
Westward Christmas
(Montana Mail Order brides Book 11)
Westward Visions
(Montana Mail Order brides Book 12)
Westward Secrets
(Montana Mail Order brides Book 13)
Westward Changes
(Montana Mail Order brides Book 14)
Westward Heartbeat
(Montana Mail Order brides Book 15)
Westward Joy
(Montana Mail Order brides Book 16)
Westward Courage
(Montana Mail Order brides Book 17)
Westward Spirit
(Montana Mail Order brides Book 18)
Westward Fate
(Montana Mail Order brides Book 19)
Westward Hope
(Montana Mail Order brides Book 20)
Westward Wild
(Montana Mail Order brides Book 21)
Westward Sight
(Montana Mail Order brides Book 22)
Westward Horizons
(Montana Mail Order brides Book 23)

Connect With Linda

Visit my website at **www.lindabridey.com** to view my other books and to sign up to my mailing list so that you are notified about my new releases.

About Linda Bridey

LINDA BRIDEY lives in New Mexico with her three dogs; a German shepherd, chocolate Labrador retriever, and a black Pug. She became fascinated with Montana and decided to combine that fascination with her fictional romance writing. Linda chose to write about mail-order-brides because of the bravery of these women who left everything and everyone to take a trek into the unknown. The Westward series books are her first publications.

Made in the USA
Monee, IL
03 March 2021